Ember Creek

A Novel

Elle Laine

Cover illustration by Kai Degraff

*Cover design for Ember Creek created exclusively
for Elle Laine, 2026*

Published by Elle Laine

First Edition, 2026

Printed in the United States of America

ISBN (Paperback) 979-8-234-07309-9

For permissions, rights inquiries, or correspondence:
@ellelaine

Dedication

To every small town that taught me that cold shoulders and closed doors are not the welcome a person deserves.

~

I came looking for my happy ending. You didn't have one for me.

So, I wrote it.

~

Welcome to Ember Creek. This is what it was always supposed to feel like.

TABLE OF CONTENTS

Chapter 1
New Roads, Old Ghosts

The moving truck smelled like cardboard and someone else's memories.

Diane Calloway sat in the passenger seat with her knees pulled up, a lukewarm gas station coffee balanced on her thigh and a playlist she had titled — with devastating optimism — "Fresh Start" playing softly through one earbud. The other earbud dangled against her collarbone, collecting road dust. She had not been able to commit to the full stereo experience in two years. It felt like too much. Like joy was something she could only take in half doses now, rationed carefully, so she did not run out.

Outside the window, the flat sprawl of the city dissolved slowly, giving way to smaller towns, then farmland, then trees that grew taller and closer together until the highway became a two-lane road cutting through a pine forest so dense it blocked out most of the afternoon light. The world turned gold and green and breathtakingly still.

"You doing okay over there?" Pete, her cousin and reluctant moving companion, glanced at her from the driver's seat. He had the look of a man who had agreed to a two-day favor and was now realizing it would require actual emotional labor. Pete was thirty-four, a middle school gym teacher, and the closest thing Diane had to a brother. He had shown up at her apartment door at six in the morning with two egg biscuits and the posture of someone bracing for a storm.

"I'm great," Diane said, in the specific tone that meant the exact opposite.

Pete nodded slowly. "Right."

She turned back to the window. Great was not the word. Neither was fine, or okay, or any of the other single syllable lies she had been handing out for the past two years like Halloween candy to neighbors she barely knew. The truth was more complicated, harder to wrap up in a bow and present to well-meaning people who asked with their heads tilted gently to the side.

The truth was this: her name was Diane Calloway, she was thirty-one years old, she used to be a person who laughed loudly at dinner parties and cried at book endings and kissed a man named Eddie Sullivan like it was something she had been practicing her whole life for. She used to read two, sometimes three romance novels a month. She used to believe — truly, deeply, embarrassingly believe — in the kind of love that was written in those books. The slow burn. The missed chances. The moment when everything finally clicks into place.

Eddie had been her click.

And then one rainy Tuesday evening in October, a car ran a red light on Fifth and Morrison, and the click became a silence so permanent she still had not figured out how to fill it.

> *Two years, three months, and twelve days.*

Not that she was counting.

She was absolutely counting.

The truck groaned around a curve and suddenly the trees parted and there it was — Ember Creek, Colorado, population 1,400, and approximately one hundred percent not the city she had spent the last decade building a life in. The main street came into view first: a row of storefronts with wooden sign posts, a hardware store with a hand-painted elk above the door, a diner called Ruby's with a neon coffee cup blinking lazily in the window, and in between all the practical, everyday businesses — a little shop with a dark green door and gold lettering on the glass that read: The Book Nook.

Diane sat up straighter.

She had not meant to. It happened involuntarily, the way your posture improves when you walk past a bakery and the smell of something warm and yeasty catches you mid-step. Some part of her, deeper than grief, that still remembered who she used to be — that part noticed the bookstore.

"That's the one?" Pete said, nodding toward it.

"That's the one."

He slowed the truck as they rolled through town. A woman walking a golden retriever raised a hand in greeting. A man on a ladder stringing lights above his shop entrance gave them a nod. Two kids on bicycles stopped to stare with the unashamed curiosity that only children and small towns seem to permit.

"Friendly," Pete said.

"Apparently." Diane wrapped both hands around her now fully cold coffee. "The woman I spoke to when I inquired about the job — Linda — she said everyone knows everyone here within about a week."

"That sounds like heaven or a nightmare?"

Diane considered it. "Ask me again in a week."

The cabin was another six miles up a winding road that climbed into the mountain in a way that made Pete grip the steering wheel with both hands and muttering things under his breath that Diane chose not to hear. It appeared through the trees like something from a postcard — small, honest, built from dark timber with a covered porch and a stone chimney that she could already picture breathing smoke into the cold mountain air.

It was the most alone place she had ever agreed to live in.

She loved it immediately and completely.

They spent three hours unloading, Pete making increasingly dramatic commentary about the elevation and his knees while Diane directed boxes to rooms with the focused efficiency of someone who had spent weeks planning this moment down to which shelf her coffee mugs would live on. When it was finished, they stood on the porch in the early dark with cold beers and the kind of silence that mountains specialize in — thick and full and all the way down.

"Diane," Pete said finally.

"Don't."

"I just want to say—"

"Pete. I know. I love you. Thank you. Now please don't make me cry because I just arranged my bookshelf in a very emotionally satisfying way and I don't want to ruin that energy."

He looked at her for a long moment. Then he raised his beer. "To Ember Creek."

She clinked hers against it. "To fresh starts."

She said it as steadily as she could. She almost believed it.

After Pete left the next morning, after the sound of the truck had faded down the mountain road and the silence rushed back into the space it left, Diane stood in the center of her small living room and breathed. The morning light came through the windows at a low angle, cutting across the wooden floor in wide golden bars. A single box still sat unpacked in the corner — the one she had labeled with just her own handwriting and no description, the one Pete had not touched and she had not explained.

She left it there.

She put on her jacket, walked out the front door, and started down the mountain toward the town.

> *One step at a time, Di. That is all it is.*

The trees were spectacular. She had not expected that, not really, had not prepared herself for the way the pine forest smelled in the early morning, like cold air and earth and something that had no name in the city. Her boots crunched through a thin skin of frost on the path. A bird she could not identify made a sound in the branches above her — three descending notes, then silence, then three again, like it was practicing a sentence it kept getting wrong.

She walked all the way into town.

She pushed open the green door of The Book Nook.

The bell above it rang twice — a gentle ding ding — and the smell hit her first: paper, coffee, and the warmth of a small room full of books. She stopped just inside the door and closed her eyes for three seconds.

"You must be Diane."

The woman behind the counter was in her late fifties, with silver-threaded hair pinned in a loose knot and reading glasses pushed up on her forehead like a second pair of eyes. She had the face of someone who had read every book in the shop and had opinions about all of them.

"I'm Linda. Welcome to Ember Creek, honey. Welcome to The Book Nook. And more importantly —" she came around the counter and pressed a ceramic mug into Diane's hands "— welcome to the best cup of chamomile on this side of the Rockies."

Diane looked down at the mug. Then back up at Linda.

And for the first time in longer than she could remember, she felt something unclench in the center of her chest. Not healed. Not whole. Just — loosened, slightly. Like a knot that had been pulled so tight it had almost become part of the rope, and someone had simply pressed their thumb into it and said: here. Start here.

"Thank you," Diane said.

She meant it in more ways than she had words for.

Chapter 2

The Things She Carried

The box in the corner stayed packed for eleven days.

Diane was aware of this in the specific, sideways way that you become aware of a bruise — not looking at it directly but always knowing exactly where it is, navigating carefully around the edges of it in every room you move through. She shelved her cookbooks. She arranged her collection of mismatched mugs by size and emotional significance. She hung the watercolor of the coast that her college roommate had painted, the one that had been in every apartment she had ever lived in, in the spot by the kitchen window where morning light would find it.

The box stayed where it was.

It was labeled, in Eddie's handwriting, because she had handed him the marker while she read the packing tape instructions aloud, which was the sort of ridiculous division of labor they had always fallen into naturally. He had written: DIANE'S BOOKS — THE GOOD ONES. Beneath that, because Eddie Sullivan had never been able to resist, he had added a tiny drawing of a heart.

It was the last box she would ever watch him label.

She had not known that, standing in the kitchen of their apartment, reading him the tape instructions in a voice making a bad impression of a flight attendant. She had not known so many things.

So, the box was here now, in the corner of her Ember Creek cabin, and Diane gave it the same respectful distance she would give a sleeping cat — present, acknowledged, untouched.

She worked at The Book Nook on Tuesdays, Thursdays, and Saturdays. It was a gentle schedule, deliberately chosen. Linda had been warm and practical about it, the way experienced women in small towns often are about the needs of newcomers who have arrived carrying things they do not yet know how to set down.

"Come in when you can," Linda had said on the phone, months ago, when Diane had applied for the position. "This isn't a place that demands. It's a place that welcomes."

Diane had wanted to cry at that. She had, a little, after she hung up. Quietly, into a dish towel, because the grief had this habit of ambushing her when kindness arrived unexpectedly.

On Tuesday, her first official shift, she arrived fifteen minutes early and spent those minutes on the sidewalk outside, watching the town go about its morning. A man in overalls carried a crate of something into Ruby's Diner. A woman jogged past with two dogs who had deeply mismatched energy — one straining at the leash, the other appearing to be philosophically opposed to the whole enterprise. The hardware store owner swept his steps with the methodical satisfaction of someone who had been doing it for thirty years and intended to do it for thirty more.

Everything was unhurried. That was the word that kept presenting itself — unhurried. Like time moved at a different rate here, something just a few degrees slower than the city, where Diane had spent years in perpetual motion, always five minutes behind some destination.

She took a breath of cold mountain air and went inside.

Linda was already there, arranging a display of new arrivals near the front window. She had taste — Diane noticed this immediately. The books were arranged not by genre or alphabet but by some more intuitive logic: books that felt like winter mornings near the fireplace, books that felt like the first warm day in March, books that felt like three a.m. and being very, very awake. Diane did not say any of this aloud. She was not ready to be that person yet.

"Counter, register, tea station," Linda said, gesturing around the shop in a three-point tour. "The regular customers will tell you everything else you need to know. Do not try to stop them. Just nod along and ask follow-up questions."

"What kind of follow-up questions?"

"'Oh really?' works for about eighty percent of situations. 'And then what?' covers another fifteen. The last five percent is advanced material — you'll develop instincts."

Diane almost laughed. It came out as something gentler — a short exhale through the nose, the kind of thing that was a laugh's smaller, more cautious cousin. But she felt it, which was something.

The customers began to arrive midmorning: a retired schoolteacher named Dorothy who wanted the latest installment of a mystery series and had thoughts — strong, detailed, unasked-for thoughts — about the author's decision to kill off a secondary character in book four. A young father with an infant strapped to his chest who needed a picture book about trucks and spent ten minutes asking questions about the books' educational value while the baby slept through all of it, entirely unbothered. Two women around Diane's age, Carla and Beth, who bought nothing but spent forty-five minutes looking at things, and who introduced themselves with the easy warmth of people who had grown up in a place where strangers eventually became neighbors.

"You're the one who moved into the Harmon cabin," Carla said. It was not a question.

"Is that what they call it?"

"Jim Harmon built it in the eighties, used it for hunting seasons for about twenty years, then decided he was too old for hunting and too attached to the cabin to sell it outright, so he started renting it. Before you there was a retired geologist who lived there for three years and spoke too exactly no one." She said this without judgment. "You're already doing better.

You've been here eleven days and you're working at The Book Nook."

"Word travels fast."

"In Ember Creek?" Beth smiled. "Word travels before you've finished saying it."

They bought nothing, as mentioned, but they left their numbers in the back of a receipt and told Diane that Ruby's Diner did a Tuesday soup special and she was invited. Diane took the receipt and put it in her jacket pocket and told herself she would think about it.

She would think about it, and she would go, because that is what fresh starts required — the terrifying act of saying yes to things before you were ready.

After her shift, she walked back up to the cabin as the light shifted to the particular amber of late afternoon in the mountains. She built a fire with the reasonable competence of someone who had watched approximately thirty instructional videos and was applying the knowledge for the first time in an actual fireplace. It took four attempts. The fire, when it finally caught, was small and a little uncertain, and Diane sat in front of it on the rug with her knees pulled to her chest and said to no one:

"I'm here, Eddie. I'm trying."

> *She could almost hear him. That's my girl.*

She pressed her forehead to her knees and let herself cry for exactly six minutes. She knew it was six minutes because she had started setting a timer — not to limit the grief, but because the open-endedness of it used to terrify her, the sense that once she started, she might not be able to find the other side. The timer was a promise. This has an end. You will still be here when it stops.

The timer went off. Diane wiped her face with her sleeve. The fire crackled warmly.

She went to bed.

She would try to unpack the box tomorrow. If she couldn't she would try to make progress on everything else.

Chapter 3

The Bell Rings

It happened on a Thursday in the deep blue cold of early December.

Diane had settled into something that felt, if not like routine, then at least like the rough outline of one — a sketch of a life that she was slowly filling in with color. She rose with the mountain light, walked the trail through the pines before the frost had fully retreated, arrived at The Book Nook smelling faintly of cold air and the vanilla-scented hand cream she'd bought at the pharmacy because Linda had one on the counter and Diane had spent four minutes standing in front of the lotion section trying to remember what she used to smell like before grief took up so much space.

She had come in on her days off too. She had not meant to — it was not a planned development. But the cabin, while beautiful, was quiet in a way that could go from peaceful to heavy with little warning, and The Book Nook occupied a particular frequency that her nervous system had begun to recognize as safe. She was not reading. She had made herself no promises about reading. She was simply present, in a room full of books, drinking tea, listening.

The gossip of Ember Creek was, it turned out, exceptional.

There was the ongoing saga of whether the Martinson family's rooster was technically a noise ordinance violation (it was, legally, but Doug Martinson was on the town council, so the situation was "under review"). There was the question of whether the new ski resort expansion would go through, which divided the town into two camps with the fervor of a much more serious conflict. There was Dorothy, the retired schoolteacher, who had opinions about absolutely everything and delivered them with the devastating confidence of someone who had spent thirty years telling children they were wrong.

Diane sat in the armchair in the back corner with her tea, a notepad she never wrote anything in, and the expression of a person browsing the shelves. She was not browsing the shelves. She was listening to every single word. She had not been this consistently entertained since she and Eddie used to play a game at restaurants where they invented backstories for people at nearby tables.

Diane blinked. She pressed her thumb into the side of her mug as she felt the sting of that feeling, the one where she misses him. That is the feeling she tries so hard to avoid because no matter how much time seems to pass, the void of his absence does not. She wraps her hands around her mug, takes a deep breath in, and cannot help but think to herself,

Eddie, come back to me, I do not want to do this thing called life without you.

Diane sat in the silence, staring out at the snow knowing that no matter how many times she demanded he return, he would not.

She looked up and out the front window at the snow that was coming down in the slow, solemn way it does in the mountains — not city snow, which was brief and apologetic and turned to slush by noon. Mountain snow meant something. It settled in and it stayed with you.

The shop had a pleasant mid-morning quiet. Linda was behind the counter writing in the order ledger. Dorothy had come and gone, leaving a book review and a verdict on the rooster situation in her wake. Carla had stopped by to pick up something for her daughter and asked Diane if she had tried the cinnamon rolls at Ruby's yet, and when Diane said not yet, Carla had pressed her hand to her chest in theatrical dismay and said "Diane. Honey. That has to change this week."

Diane smiled. It was getting easier — the smiling. More like a reflex again, less like something she had to consciously construct.

She was watching the snow fall in long peaceful curtains past the window when the bell rang.

Ding ding.

She looked up the way she always did when the bell rang — it was involuntary by now, the Pavlovian response of a woman who had decided that watching people enter a bookstore was the most sustainable form of entertainment available to her. She looked up, she noted the visitor with interest, she returned to her tea. That was the routine.

This time, she looked up and did not return to her tea.

The man who came through the door was tall — the kind of tall that registers as presence before you have had time to process the individual details. He moved like someone who worked with his hands, a certain easy physicality in the way he navigated the space between the door and the front counter. His hair was light brown and slightly too long, curling at the collar in the way hair does when a man has other things on his mind than getting it cut. He was wearing khaki carpenter pants with the pockets and the loops and, crucially — and Diane noticed this with the attention to detail she usually reserved for books — smears of paint across one thigh and along the side of the left leg. Not fresh paint. Working paint. The paint of someone who had been somewhere doing something and had come directly from that place without stopping to change.

His flannel was black with a light grey checkered pattern across the arms. The collar was open.

He walked to the counter and said something to Linda that Diane, from her corner, could not hear over the soft ambient music and the commentary going on inside her own head, which had abruptly woken from its usual muted state and begun narrating at considerable speed.

Linda went to the back room. The man stood at the counter and looked at the display of new arrivals near the register with the neutral, pleasant expression of someone comfortable in their own stillness. He was not performing the waiting. He was just — waiting. There was a quality to it that Diane found she could not look away from.

Linda reappeared with a wrapped package. She slid it across the counter. The man picked it up, said something, and then turned toward the door.

"Thanks for coming by, Brian," Linda said warmly. "Tell Susan I said hello and hope she's doing well!"

Brian. His name was Brian.

He turned back toward Linda with a smile — the first full-face view Diane had had, and she was not prepared for it. He was not movie-star handsome in any dramatic or unsettling way. He was handsome in the way that the mountain was beautiful — just there, present, complete, not asking you to make a case for it. Fair skin, deep-set blue eyes, and the scruff of a man who had forgotten to shave, or decided he would get to it eventually, which was somehow more appealing than either extreme.

"I'll be sure to let her know," he said to Linda.

And then he turned back toward the door, and in doing so, his gaze swept naturally across the shop — the ordinary survey of a man checking the room — and it landed on Diane.

She did not look away in time.

She had been staring, openly, in the uncomplicated way you stare at things when you are sitting alone in the corner of a shop and have forgotten that the subjects of your observation are three-dimensional and capable of looking back.

Brian's eyes met hers.

He smiled. Not a complicated smile. Just — easy. An acknowledgment. A small, genuine thing, the way you smile at someone in a shop when you happen to catch their eye, as if to say: hello, there you are, have a good day.

He reached for the door handle.

The bell rang.

Ding ding.

And Diane, who had been in the process of constructing a return smile, suddenly realized she had been staring at this man for the better part of three minutes with her tea forgotten in her hands and her face doing what her face decided to do without her permission. The smile she produced was — according to the brief horrified review she would conduct later in the cabin bathroom mirror — a smile only in the most generous technical interpretation of the word. Her left eyebrow had done something. Her mouth had arrived at an expression that suggested she had been asked to smile while simultaneously receiving some unsettling news.

Brian stepped through the door.

The bell rang twice more — cheerful, oblivious, completely unbothered.

Diane turned to face the window and watched, through the glass, as his figure moved down the sidewalk and dissolved into the snow. She stared at the empty space where he had been.

Diane looked up at Linda, who was writing in her ledger again with the serene expression of a woman who had noticed everything and said nothing.

"Linda," Diane said carefully, "Who is Susan?"

Linda's pen paused, "Brian's grandmother, sweetheart. Lives up on Birch Road. Lovely woman. Broke her hip last spring. Brian moved here from Denver to take care of her."

"Oh," said Diane.

"Mm," said Linda.

Diane turned back to the window. The snow was coming down in its slow and purposeful way, covering the sidewalk where Brian had just walked with a thin, fresh layer of white, as if the town itself were already writing over the moment, ready to start again.

She told herself she was simply being neighborly. Curious about the community, the way one is when new to a small town.

She told herself this all the way home and was halfway convinced by the time she reached the cabin.

Chapter 4

Research

It began, as most inadvisable things do, with what she told herself was a perfectly innocent question.

She asked Linda, on her next shift, whether Brian was originally from Ember Creek or if he had moved here as an adult. She framed it in the context of a broader, anthropological interest in the town's population patterns. This was not convincing, even to her.

"Denver," Linda said, with the comfortable efficiency of a woman who knew every person in town's origin story and had been waiting to be asked. "Moved here about eight months ago. He is a carpenter — well, carpenter, painter, contractor, whatever needs doing. Half the renovations in town over the last year have been Brian's work. Fixed Dorothy's back porch, repainted the facade on the hardware store, built the Coopers a whole addition on their place up near the ski road."

"He seems — capable," Diane offered.

"He's lovely," Linda said, with simple, pointed directness. "Quiet. Does not push. But when you talk to him, you have his full attention. You know the type?"

Diane did, in the abstract sense. She did not confirm this.

"And Susan? His grandmother?" She was committed now. There was no walking it back.

"Oh, Susan Henderson is a treasure. Used to run the garden club, before her hip. Sharp as anything. She orders two books a month, always romance." Linda said this last word with a particular warmth, and Diane felt the familiar armor slide up reflexively. "Brian picks them up for her every time. Never misses. Shows up within a day of the order being ready."

Diane made a neutral sound. She was filing all of this in a mental folder she refused to label.

The research — she continued to not call it this — was also conducted via other, less direct channels.

Carla was an excellent resource, primarily because she had the generous and entirely genuine quality of someone who loved talking about the people she loved, and she had lived in Ember Creek her whole life. Over cinnamon rolls at Ruby's (Diane had finally gone; they were, as advertised, a revelation), Carla covered, entirely without prompting, a comprehensive overview of Brian's tenure in town.

"He's been here since March. He is doing the renovations on the old Johnson place now — you know the one, up past the mill. He does stuff for my dad sometimes when the farm equipment needs attention. He does not overcharge. Which in a small town, let me tell you — that matters."

"He sounds like a good person," Diane said.

"He's a great person. We have been trying to get him out to things — the harvest festival, the tree lighting — and he comes, but he is..." Carla paused, rotating her mug in her hands. "He's a little bit in his own world. Not unfriendly, just contained. Like he's thinking about something else."

Diane thought about the way he had looked at the book display while waiting for Linda. Like a man who was comfortable being exactly where he was, without needing to perform it.

"He's single, by the way," Beth said from across the table, without looking up from her soup.

Diane said: "I didn't ask."

Carla and Beth exchanged a look that communicated twelve sentences in the time it took to blink.

"Of course," said Carla.

"Obviously," said Beth.

Diane redirected the conversation to the rooster situation, which had been the town's most pressing civic matter for the better part of three months and showed absolutely no signs of resolution, and felt the back of her neck go warm in a way she blamed entirely on the soup.

The facts, as she had absorbed them from her corner armchair over several weeks of attentive listening, were these: a rooster named Gerald — owned by Doug and Patsy Martinson, who kept a half-acre property on the east side of Millbrook Lane — had taken to announcing himself at four-fifteen in the morning with a consistency that several of his neighbors described as personal.

Gerald was not quiet. Gerald was not intermittent. Gerald was, in the specific language of the formal noise complaint filed by three households in October, "a sustained and unreasonable disruption to the peace and reasonable sleep expectations of the surrounding residential area," a sentence that Dorothy had reportedly written herself and that read, as Ruby put it, like it had been composed in court clothes.

The problem, the one that had kept the matter in a state of unresolved limbo since the complaint was filed, was Doug Martinson. Doug Martinson was, as Carla had explained to Diane, not just on it — he chaired the zoning and ordinance subcommittee, which meant that the man responsible for adjudicating noise complaints was the same man whose rooster was generating them, a conflict of interest so obvious that it had been raised, documented, and then procedurally set aside twice in consecutive meetings on the grounds that Doug had recused himself from the vote while somehow remaining the one who scheduled the agenda.

Dorothy had called this "masterwork of bureaucratic self-preservation" at sufficient volume that it had been noted in the meeting minutes.

The Martinsons, for their part, maintained that Gerald was a heritage breed Wyandotte rooster with a documented lineage and that his presence on their property predated two of the three complaining households by several years, which was either irrelevant or deeply relevant depending on which side of Millbrook Lane you lived on. Henry Baker had circulated a petition. Dorothy had signed it first. A counter-petition, organized by Patsy Martinson with the support of a surprisingly robust coalition of Gerald sympathizers, had appeared within the week. The town, which generally united on most things, had divided on the rooster with the cheerful fervor it usually reserved for the ski resort debate, and Linda had quietly removed the comment box from the shop counter after Gerald-related opinions had begun appearing in it unprompted. The Gerald small town drama was juicy and one of Diane's favorite topics to listen to.

~

Diane started noticing Brian around town.

This was partly inevitable — Ember Creek was not a city where you could lose track of someone. But it was also, she suspected, partly a function of the fact that she was now, against her better judgment, looking.

She saw his truck parked outside the hardware store on a Tuesday. A dark green pickup, older, with a tool rack in the bed and a faded sticker on the rear window that she could not make out from her angle. She considered walking closer to see what it said, then considered what she was actually doing and crossed the street.

She saw him on a Saturday, coming out of Ruby's with a to-go cup and a paper bag, the collar of his flannel up against the cold, squinting slightly against the wind with an expression of amiable patience, as if the weather were an acquaintance whose behavior he'd long since accepted. He did not see her. She was on the other side of the street and walked past at what she calculated was a natural pace that absolutely was not adjusted to avoid being seen.

She spent the walk home having a conversation with herself about the difference between being curious about a neighbor — which was normal and human — and whatever this was — which was something else.

The conversation within herself reached no useful conclusions and left her understanding nothing except her curiosity was becoming more than she anticipated. Diane was not ready to accept the new development of her interest, but she was not shying away from it either.

That night, she called Pete.

"I think I might be losing my mind a little bit," she said.

"On a scale from 'thinking about buying a second coffee maker' to 'actively considering a tattoo,' where are we?"

"Somewhere in between." She was sitting on the porch in a blanket with the night pressing in from the tree line, the stars doing the mountain thing they did — more of them, brighter, closer. "There's a guy."

"A guy," Pete said carefully.

"In town. He came into the bookstore. I saw him. I've — I may have asked some questions about him."

"Questions?"

"Linda. Carla. Beth. Standard inquiries."

Pete was quiet for a moment. "Diane."

"I know."

"That's — Di, that's really good."

"I don't know if it is. I feel—" She stopped. Tried to locate the word. "I feel like I'm betraying him. Eddie. Like, what am I doing being curious about someone? It hasn't been long enough."

"How long is long enough?"

"I don't know. More than this."

"Says who?"

She did not have an answer.

"I'm not trying to push," Pete said. "I'm just — you don't have to perform grief for anyone, Diane. Including yourself. Eddie loved you. He would not have wanted this to be the rest of your story."

> *Tell me the best version of the story, Di. His voice, so specific. How it lifted at the end of sentences, like everything he said was an invitation.*

She pressed her palm flat against her chest.

"I haven't even spoken to this man," she said. "I'm catastrophizing over a stranger."

"That's deeply on brand for you."

"Thank you, Pete."

"Anytime!"

She said goodnight and sat outside for a while longer, watching the sky. A single question circled in her mind, not anxious exactly, just — persistent, the way the bird in the pines repeated its three notes over and over, as if hoping someone would eventually answer.

Why was she so curious about this one?

She did not know.

She went inside. She made tea. She looked at the box in the corner.

She was not ready to open it yet.

But she touched it, for the first time, on the way past.

Just a quick press of her fingers against the cardboard.

"I haven't forgotten you."

Chapter 5

The Winter Festival and the Art of Missing

Ember Creek's Annual Winter Festival took place on the second Saturday of December, and no one thought of warning Diane how seriously the town took it.

"When you say 'festival,'" she said to Linda, watching her rearrange the front window display to accommodate a small cluster of hand-painted wooden ornaments the shop was selling as a fundraiser, "what are we talking about, exactly? Is it a — like, a street fair type of situation?"

Linda straightened up and turned to look at Diane with the expression of a woman presented with a question so fundamentally insufficient it required a moment of recalibration. "Diane. The Winter Festival is Ember Creek. It is for three days. There's ice sculpting. There is a ski race. There's the bonfire on Saturday night that Tom Kettley has hosted for thirty years and if you are not there with a thermos by eight p.m. you will never hear the end of it."

"Three days?"

"And the cinnamon rolls at Ruby's on Sunday morning to close it out are — I cannot overstate this — transcendent. Carla will agree."

Carla, who happened to be in the shop at that moment pretending to look at the rotating paperback rack but actually tracking every word of this conversation, looked up and said: "Come. Diane. This is non-negotiable."

Diane knew this was not something she could get out of and made the mental note that she would go and do her best to be a part of the town's traditions.

On Saturday, she layered herself in every warm garment she'd brought from the city — which was not quite enough for mountain December, a fact she had been refusing to acknowledge until the walk down the hill disabused her of it completely — and arrived on Main Street to find it completely transformed. Strings of white lights ran the length of every storefront from one end of the block to the other. An ice sculptor was at work in the town square with a chainsaw and a focus that Diane found genuinely thrilling to watch. A bluegrass trio was set up near the diner, playing something that made your feet do things without your permission.

Children were everywhere — a current of small people in bright coats, red-cheeked and screaming with the joy of cold-weather freedom. An actual horse-drawn sleigh was making slow loops around the square, which Diane watched with delight.

"Told you," Carla said, appearing at her elbow with two cups of something hot and handing one over.

"This is absurd," Diane said, meaning it as a compliment.

"This is Ember Creek." Carla touched her cup to Diane's. "Welcome, officially."

She spent the morning moving through it all with Carla and Beth, stopping at craft booths, watching the children's ski race that went somewhat off-script when one participant decided partway down the hill that he'd prefer not to race after all and sat down in the snow with dignified resolve, resulting in a traffic situation that required parental intervention. She got a mug of spiced cider from the booth run by the high school's music boosters and stood near the ice sculpture to watch the chainsaw artist transform a block of ice into something that was, improbably, an incredibly good bear.

She was watching the bear emerge from the ice when she felt, with no logical explanation whatsoever, the prickle of being observed.

She turned.

He was twenty feet away, near the edge of the square, talking to an older man Diane did not know. He was wearing a dark navy coat over his flannel, a grey knit hat pulled low, he was holding a cup and laughing at something the other man had said — a real laugh, full and easy, the kind that rearranged a person's face.

Then his gaze shifted, the way it does when you feel someone looking at you, and he saw her.

Diane did not look away this time.

She stood there with her cider and her unfortunate lack of a prepared facial expression and they simply — looked at each other. For about four seconds. Which is, in the economy of charged eye contact between strangers, approximately forty years.

Brian's expression did not change dramatically. There was just a — a slight something. Recognition. He raised his cup — the most minimal and yet somehow the most devastating of acknowledgments — and then the older man said something, and before Diane could return the gesture, Brian turned away, and the moment closed. Diane stood there trying to connect the moment to her thoughts but before she could she heard: "What was that?" as Carla materialized at her side.

"Nothing."

"That was Brian Henderson."

"I know who Brian Henderson is," Diane said, in a tone of voice that she immediately recognized as far too invested to belong to someone who only knew who Brian Henderson was in the most basic, neighborly sense.

Carla said nothing as she sipped her cider, but her silence was incredibly loud.

The bonfire that evening was everything Linda had promised. Tom Kettley's farm field on the edge of town, a fire the size of a small building, the entire population of Ember Creek arranged around it in concentric rings of lawn chairs, blankets, and thermoses. Someone was playing a fiddle, and the stars were out in their usual, majestic mountain form.

Diane sat between Carla and Beth with her borrowed thermos of hot chocolate and let herself be held by the warmth of it — the fire, the music, the company, the simple comfort of being among people under an open sky. She was not thinking about anything for once, she was just here, in this, which was a thing she was getting better at and found the peace in her mind to be like an old friend she reunited with.

As Diane took in the evening's sights, across the fire, through the wavering orange light, Brian appeared.

He was standing at the back of the crowd, coat on, hands in pockets, looking into the fire with an expression she could not fully read in the distance. Not unhappy — just somewhere else, the way people go sometimes when the warmth and the light push them gently inward instead of out.

She knew that feeling.

> *She had spent two years inside that feeling.*

Then someone said something to him —
a man she had seen at the hardware
store— and Brian came back, answered,
laughed that laugh again. Present again.
Returned from wherever he had been.

Diane looked back at the fire as she
realized she was staring at Brian like a
total creep across the way and redirected
her attention back to the fire.

She did not tell Carla or Beth what she
was thinking. She was not sure she could
articulate it.

She was thinking about people who
carried things quietly, and how you could
sometimes recognize it in others before
you had said a single word.

Chapter 6

Town Property

By the time the new year arrived, Diane and Brian had still not spoken.

This was becoming, in the opinion of various interested parties in Ember Creek — which is to say, everyone — a situation.

It began in December with Linda's observation to Dorothy that the new girl at the shop and the Henderson boy had made eyes at each other a notable number of times. Dorothy had relayed this to her Thursday morning walking group with the careful specificity of a woman taking depositions. The walking group had dispersed the information to their respective households and social circles over the course of a weekend, and by the following Monday it had achieved the status of an ongoing narrative with a growing invested audience.

The fact that neither Brian nor Diane was aware of this audience made it, somehow, more compelling.

"They just look at each other," Carla said to Beth over coffee at Ruby's, which was not so much a private conversation as a performance with witnesses, since Ruby's had excellent acoustics and no true strangers. "Every time. He sees her, she sees him, they have this — moment — and then they both just turn and walk away."

"It's excruciating," Beth said.

"In the best way."

"Completely."

This conversation was reported back to Linda by Ruby herself, who had been within earshot, as Ruby usually was, because it was her diner and she had views on most things happening in it.

Linda filed it under: developing well. Proceed with patience.

~

January in Ember Creek brought two town events that Diane attended in the spirit of her ongoing fresh start project, which she was running with the determination and occasional despair of a woman renovating a house while living in it.

The first was the New Year's potluck at the community center, which Diane attended, bearing a pasta dish she had made three times to get right, and which was received with the warm, specific approval of a small town that means it when they say it is good. She wore the green sweater that Eddie had always liked — she had put it on automatically and then stood in front of the mirror, deciding whether to take it off, and then left it on, because she was getting better at letting things be both sad and slowly getting better.

The community center was warm, loud, and crowded, which Diane had not anticipated. She'd been picturing something modest and instead was presented with every household in town, four folding tables of food, a raffle for a gift basket from The Book Nook that Linda was running with the enjoyment of a woman in her natural element, and a local band playing covers from a small stage in the corner.

She was laughing at something Dorothy was saying about the rooster situation's latest development — a formal petition which had collected forty-two signatures — when she looked up and saw him at the food table.

Brian, filling a plate with the focused deliberation of a man who takes potluck seriously. He had traded the carpenter pants for dark jeans, same flannel family, this one navy. He was standing next to an older woman in a wheelchair who was directing the plate-filling with considerable authority — pointing at items, gesturing, shaking her head at one thing and nodding emphatically at another.

Susan. His grandmother. Diane knew this immediately.

She also noticed — she could not, not notice — that Brian was doing every bit of it with ease. He was not making a show of patience or care. He was just there, paying attention, letting his grandmother have her opinion about the green bean situation. He was showing up for Susan, and that thought brought a warm familiarity that brought a knot to Diane's stomach as she thought about it.

> *The man who shows up. That was what Eddie had called it, talking about the kind of person he wanted to be. You don't have to be the biggest or loudest thing in the room. You just have to be the one who shows up.*

Diane looked away before Brian could look up. She was getting much better at catching herself in the creeper stares and correcting herself before being caught in the act. The thought of being caught mid-stare by Brian brought a horrifying feeling to the pit of her stomach but then she found herself giggling a bit for being so silly about a guy. He is just a guy, she reminded herself.

Across the room, Linda caught her eye and smiled with the serene, unhurried expression of someone who was not at all concerned that this was taking a while, because she had complete confidence in the eventual outcome.

Diane gave her a look. Linda's smile did not diminish.

~

The second event was the January outdoor market, a smaller affair — vendors with winter goods and warm beverages, the town's collective commitment to finding reasons to gather even when the temperature was trying to discourage the whole idea.

Diane went with Carla and spent twenty minutes at a soap-maker's booth smelling things, then bought a candle from a woman named Jo who made them in her garage and had seventeen different varieties organized by mood rather than scent. She picked one labeled "somewhere new," which was cedar and something lighter underneath — chamomile, maybe — and held it all the way home.

At the market, she saw Brian twice.

The first time: at the baker's booth, paying for something, having what appeared to be a very pleasant conversation with old Henry Baker who was eighty-one and could talk to anyone about anything without drawing a breath.

The second time: right next to her, separated by approximately four feet and the booth of a woman selling knitted hats, as they both stood examining the same display. Diane registered this a half second before he did and spent that half second making a rapid series of decisions: do not look up immediately, look up naturally, produce a reasonable expression, be a normal human person who has not memorized his truck's parking spots.

She looked up. Then he looked up.

Four feet. Direct eye contact. The knitted hat seller choosing this moment to go to her car for more inventory, leaving them in a pocket of unusual stillness.

Diane smiled. She was certain it was a better smile than the first one. She had been practicing expressions in the mirror, privately and with great personal embarrassment, specifically to avoid a repeat of the bookstore incident.

Brian smiled back. He opened his mouth. Something was about to happen. The four feet between them were about to become something else entirely.

"BRIAN!" A man's voice, from somewhere behind her. "Hey, Brian, you've got a second? Toms got a question about the barn project—"

Brian glanced over her shoulder, and the open moment sealed itself shut like a book you did not mean to close.

"Yeah," he called back. He looked at Diane once more — and there was something in it, something apologetic, or maybe that was the winter light playing tricks — and then he was moving past her. The hat seller returned with her inventory, and Carla reappeared at Diane's elbow asking if she had seen the honey booth.

Diane stared at the knitted hats for a moment.

"You okay?" Carla asked.

"Yes," Diane said. "Do you think this one would look good on me?" She held up a bright orange hat with a pom-pom the size of a tennis ball on top.

Carla studied it. "If your goal is to be seen from space, absolutely!"

Diane put the hat on. It was terrible. She bought it immediately.

Small joys. You took them where you found them.

Chapter 7

What Grandmother Susan Knows

Susan Henderson had broken her hip in April, moved to the ground floor of her own house in May, and by June had developed a network of information so comprehensive that Brian sometimes suspected she knew things before they happened.

"The woman at the book shop," she said, without preamble or context, while Brian was fixing the cabinet under the bathroom sink that had been making a noise she described as "a complaint."

Brian's head was under the cabinet. "Which woman?"

"The new one. Diane. From the city. Linda hired her in November."

"Okay."

"Have you spoken to her?"

"Gran."

"It's a simple question."

He emerged from under the cabinet, sat back on his heels, and looked at her with the expression he reserved for these conversations — fond, slightly worn, entirely aware he was not going to win. Susan was in the doorway in her wheelchair with a cup of tea and the patient demeanor of a woman who has learned to conduct interrogations from a seated position without losing any authority.

"I've seen her at the shop," he said. "We haven't spoken."

"Why not?"

"Because I was picking up your books and leaving."

"You could have introduced yourself."

"I could have."

"Brian."

"Susan."

She gave him the look — the one that had been working on him since he was nine years old and had significantly more authority than the equivalent parental version because grandmothers, uniquely, have nothing left to prove. "I want you to be happy," she said.

He went back under the cabinet. "I am happy."

"You're fine. There's a difference."

He adjusted something that made a clunk noise, which he was confident was an improvement. "Gran. I moved here to take care of you. Not to — I am not looking for anything. I'm where I want to be."

"I didn't say you were looking. I said you should say hello to the woman."

"Based on what?"

"Based on the fact that Linda says she's lovely and she misses the city in the way that people do when they've left it for a reason, and she takes long walks in the woods by herself and she's been sitting in the back corner of the bookshop for two months listening to Dorothy's gossip with this expression like someone who'd been starving and found a meal. And she looked at you."

Brian went very still under the cabinet.

"She looked at you the way—" Susan paused, choosing her words with the care of someone wielding something precise, "The way a woman looks when she's trying very hard *not* to look."

Brian came out from under the cabinet. He sat on the bathroom floor and looked at his grandmother.

"You got all of that from Linda?"

"Linda. Dorothy. Carla. Beth." She sipped her tea. "I also have my own sources."

"You have sources."

"I've lived in this town for sixty years, Brian. The information finds me."

He wiped his hands on a rag and said nothing.

"She lost someone," Susan said, more gently. "Her person. A while ago. Linda told me, in a careful way, because Linda is discreet — which, coming from me, is the highest possible praise."

Brian looked at the floor tile. It needed re-grouting in the corner; he made a mental note.

"I know about that," Susan said. "The kind of loss that makes you start again somewhere new, because the old place has the shape of someone in it that you can't stop seeing."

He looked up at her.

"Your grandfather passed, you were four. You wouldn't remember." She said this with the equanimity of forty years of making peace with something. "I stayed in this town because the town was him, in a way. But I understand why some people have to leave their town."

Brian nodded.

"I'm not telling you to fall in love with the woman," Susan said. "I'm telling you to say hello. She is new. She is alone out in that cabin. And you are—" a small, careful pause "—you're also a little bit alone, Brian, even when you're surrounded by people."

He looked at his grandmother for a long moment. She looked back with the unwavering clarity of someone who had earned the right to say these things.

"The cabinet's fixed," he said finally.

"I know you heard me."

"Yes," he said. "I heard you."

He did not say anything else. He packed up his tools, made her lunch, and watched the news with her for an hour, and when he left he kissed the top of her head, she squeezed his hand, and neither of them brought it up again.

But driving home through the early dark, Brian found himself thinking about what it might look like — saying hello. The mechanics of it. The ordinary human act that felt, for some reason he could not fully explain, like it required something he had not fully located yet.

He had moved to Ember Creek because his grandmother needed him, and that was true and real, and he did not regret a single day of it. But there was also the other thing — the thing he did not say aloud — which was that Denver had become a city of wrong turns.

He had ended a three-year relationship the fall before the move, cleanly and mutually and with the sadness of two people who cared about each other but had been heading in different directions for longer than either of them had admitted. He had been twenty-nine, then thirty, then thirty-one, doing good work and coming home to a quiet apartment and telling himself it was exactly what he wanted.

He was not sure anymore.

He drove home through the dark and parked in front of his small house and sat for a minute with the engine off, looking at nothing and thinking.

He thought about a woman in the corner of a bookshop with a tea mug and the expression of someone hearing a song they had forgotten they knew.

He thought about eyes that had met his twice now and gone sideways both times.

He thought: just say hello.

He went inside, made dinner, called his mother, and went to bed.

He would say hello, eventually.

Chapter 8

February, and the Box

She opened the box on a Sunday in February during a snowstorm.

It was not a dramatic decision — or rather, it was, but it did not feel dramatic in the moment. She had been awake early, the kind of early that winter brings without warning, when the dark outside is thick and close and there is no real reason to get up but something in you needs to move. She had made coffee. She had stood at the window. The snow was new and heavy, bending the pine branches into weighted curves, and the light it cast was that particular grey-white that softens all the edges of things.

She had looked at the box and decided to pick up the scissors and cut the tape.

His handwriting on the side: DIANE'S BOOKS — THE GOOD ONES. Below it, the small heart.

She sat on the floor in front of the box with her coffee balanced on her knee and lifted out the first book.

It was a worn paperback — the spine cracked from being read multiple times, a sliver of a bookmark still in it about two-thirds through. She had been two-thirds through this book when Eddie died. She had never learned what happened at the end, and for two years she had been certain she did not want to know. That the ending was somehow tied up in him, in the specific ordinary afternoon when she'd been reading while he cooked dinner and called out from the kitchen asking if she wanted the spicy sauce or the mild, and she'd said spicy without looking up from the page, and that was the last completely uncomplicated moment she could remember before everything changed.

> *Mild. I should have said mild and I would have gone to help him and I wouldn't have been on the couch reading when his phone rang and I wouldn't have answered it and the voice on the other end wouldn't have asked me if I was related to Edward Sullivan.*

She pressed the back of her hand to her mouth.

Then she breathed. One breath. Then another.

The grief was still there. That was not a surprise. She had stopped expecting it to vanish and started expecting it to simply — evolve. To become something she carried differently. Pete called it remodeling, which was his way. Linda, in that quiet way Linda had, called it, putting the love somewhere it could still live.

She pulled all the books out and arranged them around her on the floor.

There were twenty-two. She counted them because she was Diane and she always counted things. Some were pristine, some were loved to pieces. Two of them had Eddie's handwriting in the margins — he had borrowed them once when she was sick and bored of the television, and he had made small notes, arguing with characters, predicting plot points, writing a checkmark next to things that surprised him. She ran her thumb over his handwriting in the margin of one page.

Saw this coming from chapter two, he'd written. But in a good way.

She laughed. It came out wet, ragged, and real.

She sat with the books for a long time. She told him about Ember Creek — the snow, the people, the gossip she had been collecting like a hobby, Linda and her perfect chamomile tea, the satellite stars. She told him about the box in the corner and how it had taken her three months to get to this point.

Di. You have to keep reading. You love it. Don't let me be the reason you stopped.

"You're not a reason. You are an exception," she told the snow out the window.

She picked up the book she had been reading that last ordinary afternoon and turned to where the bookmark was and kept going.

~

She read for four hours. The snow came down the whole time.

When she finished the book — when she got to the ending she'd waited two years for, which was exactly the ending it should have been, earned and specific and earned again — she sat with it closed on her lap and felt something she hadn't felt in so long she had to sit with it for a minute before she recognized it.

94

She was glad. She was glad she had read it. She was glad she had been here, in this cabin, on this Sunday, reading this book.

Not healed. She understood now that healed was not the destination. But — present. Here. Glad.

She put the book back in the box, but she left the lid open.

She picked up her phone and texted Linda: "I read a whole book today. Just thought you should know."

Three minutes later, Linda responded: a single heart.

Diane smiled at her phone. Then she looked at the open box, the twenty-two books, Eddie's handwriting in the margins.

"Okay," she said, to him, to herself, to the mountain and the snow and the open evening ahead of her. "Okay. I'm starting again."

She picked up the next book. She opened page one.

She read.

Chapter 9

Valentine's Day in Ember Creek (Otherwise Known as: A Lot to Handle)

Ember Creek, Diane had come to understand, treated Valentine's Day with the same cheerful, communal enthusiasm it brought to all occasions, which is to say: it went all out, and no one was spared.

The Main Street went red and pink with a thoroughness that suggested it had been planned since November — which, she later learned from Dorothy, it had. Ruby's Diner had a heart-shaped pancake special. The hardware store had a window display featuring a cupid made of actual hardware components — nuts, bolts, and washers arranged with more skill than the concept deserved. The Book

Nook had a display of romance novels arranged in a tower Linda called "The Tower of Perfectly Respectable Feelings," which made Diane laugh until she had to sit down.

She was working that Saturday. Valentine's Day itself fell on a Sunday this year, but the Saturday before was when the town was fully committed, and The Book Nook was busier than she had ever seen it. There was apparently a tradition of the men of Ember Creek waiting until forty-eight hours before to ask the bookshop to recommend something for their wives, which kept her and Linda moving at a pace that was equal parts stressful and genuinely entertaining.

"She likes mysteries, but she says they're too violent," said a man named Cal at eleven a.m., with the haunted expression of someone who had made this mistake before.

"Does she like puzzles?"

"She does the crossword every day."

"Okay." Diane moved confidently to the shelf she had been quietly building in her head since she started learning the stock. "Here. Slow burn, the mystery is intellectual not gory, and the protagonist is a woman who solves crimes using actual research." She handed it over. "It's also the first in a series. You're welcome."

Cal looked at the book. Back to Diane. Back to the book. "You just saved my life."

"Happy Valentine's Day."

Between customers, she helped Linda restock the display and found herself looking, not for the first time, at the romance section with the complicated feelings that specific category always prompted in her. She loved romance novels with the uncomplicated faith of someone who believed in what they were about. The last few years had made that harder — the stories felt like places she was locked out of, pressing her nose to the glass.

But she had read four books since the Sunday of the box. She was getting back in.

At two in the afternoon, the bell rang. Linda was in the back room. Diane was behind the counter.

She looked up.

Brian Henderson walked through the door.

Not to pick up an order. He was carrying one — a small envelope, which he placed on the counter and said: "For Susan Henderson's order? Linda said to drop it off." He paused. "I got her address wrong, apparently."

Diane looked at the envelope. She looked at Brian. He was right there. Right at the counter. Looking at her with those blue eyes that were approximately twelve inches from her face.

She had a name. She had her voice. She had rehearsed something like this.

"Happy Valentine's Day!" she said.

Okay. It was a start. But as quickly as it came out of her mouth, instant regret and worry plagued her mind and she knew it was seeping onto her face. She could not stop her face and could feel the distraught and distorted look written all over it.

"Happy Valentine's Day," Brian said with somewhat of a slight chuckle underneath it.

He had a good voice — she had heard it before, from across a room, but close it had a quality she had not anticipated. Steady. Warm. Like a cup of something.

Linda emerged from the back room, saw Brian, saw Diane, and said: "Oh, Brian! Perfect timing. Diane, Brian is Susan Henderson's grandson — he does half the work in town, honestly. Brian, this is Diane, she joined us in November." And then — because Linda was Linda — she went smoothly back to what she had been doing, leaving them in the gentlest possible construction of a conversation.

"Brian," Diane said. She already knew his name. She was saying it because she was nervous and had temporarily lost access to other words.

"Diane." A small pause. Then: "You're in the corner, usually. With tea."

She stared at him. He had noticed her. Not just at the events — here. In the shop.

"The good corner," she said. "Good light. Good gossip radius."

Something shifted in his expression — not quite a smile yet, but its precursor.

"Is the gossip good?"

"The gossip in this town is extraordinary. I've been here four months, and I have strong opinions about a rooster ordinance dispute."

And now the smile — full, easy, the one she had seen across a fire and a market square but never aimed directly at her. It was, she registered somewhere in the hinge of her chest, a very good smile.

"I've been here eight months," Brian said. "I have feelings about that rooster!"

Linda, from the back room, very pointedly said nothing.

It went on for seven minutes. Diane counted, later, running the conversation back. Seven minutes of perfectly ordinary conversation — the town, the winter, the rooster, whether Ruby's pancakes or the bakery's croissants were the superior breakfast — that felt, in the moment, neither ordinary nor perfectly calibrated.

It felt like standing at the edge of something that had its own weather.

Then someone came in the door behind Brian, and he stepped back naturally, creating space, and the moment reorganized itself into the regular shape of a busy Saturday afternoon.

"It was nice to officially meet you," Brian said.

"You too," Diane said.

He left. She watched the door swing shut.

Linda appeared at her elbow with an extremely specific expression. "Well."

"Please don't," Diane said.

"I'm not saying a word."

"You're thinking approximately six hundred words."

"That," Linda said contentedly, "is entirely possible."

Diane turned back to the counter and helped the next customer and tried, with limited success, to keep the smile off her face.

It was, she thought, an exceedingly long time since she had tried to keep a smile off her face.

She liked it. She did not fully trust it. But she liked it.

Chapter 10

The Maple Sugar Festival and Seven Near Misses

The thing about Ember Creek, Diane had decided, was that it was a town specifically engineered to put people in each other's paths.

This was not a complaint. It was an observation with personal relevance.

March brought the Maple Sugar Festival, which she had been told about by everyone she knew and which she attended with the enthusiasm of someone who had fully surrendered to the rhythm of small-town event culture. It was held in the wooded area just north of town on a cold bright Saturday that made the entire world feel clarified — the pines shining with ice melting, the air thin and clean, the kind of day that made you understand why people chose mountains over cities.

There were tapping demonstrations, syrup samples, and something called a sugar-on-snow station that involved pouring hot maple syrup onto fresh snow and eating what emerged, which was a revelation that Diane would be describing to Pete for months. There were families everywhere, and the festival energy she had come to love — that loose, unhurried pleasure of a community choosing to celebrate a small and beautiful thing together.

She saw Brian six times over the course of four hours.

She was not tracking this intentionally. She was simply aware. There is a difference. (There is arguably not a difference.)

The first time: near the tapping demonstration, where he was listening to old Henry explain the process with the attentiveness, he seemed to bring to everyone who talked to him — head tilted slightly, eyes on the speaker, no phone in hand. Diane was twenty feet away, got three feet closer when Carla steered her toward the demonstration, saw Brian, and made a natural and unhurried adjustment to her trajectory that absolutely was not avoidance.

The second time: at the syrup tasting, where they reached for the same sample cup at the same moment, resulting in a near-collision that Diane navigated by pivoting ninety degrees and pretending to be extremely interested in the label on the adjacent jar. She was sure he had seen her. She was less sure of what her face had done and was beginning to think her face had a mind of its own.

The third time: across the clearing during the children's games, where she was watching a spirited relay race and happened to look up at the exact moment he did, and they both smiled in the involuntary way you smile when you catch someone else watching the same charming thing. The relay race produced a dramatic stumble, and they both looked back at the children.

The fourth time: both at Ruby's mobile booth getting something hot to drink. They were three people apart in the line. She knew he was there. She stood very still and read the menu board with focused intensity, as though it were an exam for which she had not studied.

He did not appear to have a solution to this either.

Both made it through the line without acknowledging each other, which was an achievement of determined obliviousness that neither of them was particularly proud of.

The fifth time: Diane was coming around the corner of a row of vendor tents and nearly walked into him. He was carrying two cups of something. She stopped. He stopped. They were approximately eight inches apart.

"Hi," she said. The word came out well. She was proud of it.

"Hey," he said. Equally well-executed.

"Nice day for it," she said, with the energy of someone who has been handed words they did not want to say but gave it their best go.

"Great day," he agreed, with similar struggle.

And then the children's relay race chose this exact moment to run directly past them in a wave of small moving bodies, one of whom collided with Diane's elbow and sent her sideways, and by the time she'd steadied herself Brian had been absorbed by the passing crowd, and she was standing alone next to a tent selling beeswax candles.

She looked at the candles.

The candle seller, who had witnessed everything, said gently: "Would you like to see our spring collection?"

"Yes," said Diane. "Please. Immediately."

The sixth time: leaving. Brian was heading toward the parking area from one direction, Diane from another, and they arrived at the same exit point at the same time and shared the gap in the fence simultaneously, which required them to both slow, and step back, and do the small navigating dance of two people who are trying to let the other through, and—

"Go ahead," he said.

"No, you go—"

"After you—"

"Honestly, you—"

They both stopped. They were both smiling.

"I'll go," she said.

"Great plan," he said.

She went through the gap. He followed a step behind. The festival noise fell away behind them into the quiet parking area. She reached her car. He reached his truck, which was parked three spots over — the dark green one, the one she had identified a hundred times now.

"Good festival," he said, over the roof of the car between them.

"Really good," she said.

She got in her car. He got in his truck. She drove home through the trees thinking about absolutely nothing for forty-five solid minutes, which was to say she was thinking about everything.

~

Linda, Dorothy, Carla, Beth, and Ruby had a working group. Diane was not aware of this.

It formed organically over the winter, as things do in Ember Creek, with the low-key urgency of a neighborhood watching two people circle each other like they had both forgotten they could stop and connect.

"Something has to happen," Dorothy said at Ruby's, with the authority of a woman who had taught thirty years of children to try harder.

"Something will happen," Linda said. "We just need to create the conditions."

"When?" said Carla.

"When the time is right." Linda sipped her coffee. "And I'll know when that is."

The others had learned to trust Linda's timing.

They waited. As patiently as they could, they waited.

Chapter 11

The Setup

Linda made her move on a Tuesday in late March.

The plan was as follows, and it was elegant in the way that simple plans are — not too many moving parts, room for the moment to be its own thing once arranged.

Step one: Call Brian. Tell him Susan had a book order that needed to be picked up today — sensitive timing, could he come by in the afternoon?

Step two: Make sure Diane was working.

Step three: Call Dorothy. Dorothy would call Carla. Carla would call Beth. Beth would call Ruby. Ruby would pass it along her channel. The word would be out. The interested community would, by various routes, find reason to be in or near The Book Nook at approximately three in the afternoon.

Step four: let it be what it was.

Linda was a woman of her word and a woman of strategy, and she had been both for fifty-eight years. She had watched half this town fall in love and the other half manage heartbreak, and she knew the difference between stories that needed interference and stories that just needed a door held open.

This was the door.

She was going to hold it open.

~

By two-thirty, The Book Nook had acquired, organically and naturally, approximately fourteen customers.

This was not typical for a Tuesday in late March. Diane noticed.

"Linda," she said, during a brief gap between customers, "is there an event happening that I'm not aware of?"

"Not specifically," Linda said, which was not untrue in any technical sense.

Diane looked around. Dorothy was examining the new arrivals display with unusual focus for a woman who had already purchased everything of interest in the last six weeks. Carla and Beth were in the back corner — Diane's corner, she noted — looking at the clearance shelf but holding their browsing in the specific alert posture of people who are pretending to browse. Two other women Diane knew from the New Year's potluck were in fiction with no apparent interest in buying anything.

Something was happening.

She didn't know what, and she was distracted enough by the unusual crowd that she was behind the counter when the bell rang — ding ding — and she looked up from her register and the greeting she'd been forming in a very professional and composed way dissolved somewhere between her brain and her mouth.

Brian Henderson walked through the green door.

He was in the paint pants. The black flannel with the grey checks. His hair was doing the thing. He looked like he had come directly from a job, because he had, and there was something about a person who moves through the world in their work clothes — unhurried, unstudied — that Diane found impossible to look away from.

He came to the counter.

He was there, like right there. She was also right there, but behind the counter, which should have helped, but was not helping at all.

The professional greeting she had been constructing was gone. The words she had been using her whole life were temporarily unavailable. She was aware of approximately fourteen pairs of eyes trained on this counter with the discreet intensity of people watching a spoiler they had been waiting months for.

Brian looked at her. "Hi, I'm—"

"Yes," she said.

He paused.

"Yes, yes you are." She could hear herself. She was aware that what was coming out of her mouth was not good, but she was unable to stop it. "I know who you are. That's — silly, that you are here thinking I do not know who you are. When I clearly know exactly who you are. I mean." A breath. "Not exactly who you are. But I know you are Brian. And that is all I need to know. Because it is not like I've — I have not asked around or wondered about you. Or why you come into a bookstore. Or anything. Like that."

Silence.

Total, complete, fourteen-person silence.

Brian looked at her. His expression had moved through several phases in the last forty-five seconds that she had not had the bandwidth to track in real time. She could see in his eyes that he was making a decision — and then the decision was made, and what happened to his face was the very last thing she expected.

He laughed.

Not a polite, social laugh. A genuine one — surprised out of him, warm and real, eyes crinkling at the corners.

"Okay," he said. "Okay. I'm Brian. It's very nice to officially meet you, Diane."

She stared at him. "You know my name?"

"I asked Linda."

The silence behind them erupted. Dorothy said something that sounded like a small cheer. Carla made a sound. Linda, behind the counter to Diane's left, had the expression of a woman whose investment had just paid dividends.

Diane looked at Brian. Brian was still smiling. And as always, it was an incredibly good smile.

"So," he said, "Susan doesn't actually have a book order today, does she?"

Linda, without looking up: "She might. Check back next week."

"Right." Brian put both of his hands on the counter, leaned closer and asked, "Would it be weird to ask if you wanted to get coffee at Ruby's? Right now? Since I'm here and you're clearly... going through some things and the whole town had intentions and I think we both could use an escape plan right now."

Diane opened her mouth.

"I'm going on break," she announced to no one and everyone. She untied her apron. She came around the counter.

She did not look at Linda. If she looked at Linda, she would either cry or laugh and she could not afford either one right now.

"Let's go," she said.

The entire bookshop watched them walk out the green door together.

The bell rang.

Ding ding.

Dorothy said: "Well. Finally."

Chapter 12

Coffee at Ruby's

Rubys in the mid-afternoon was a quieter creature than its morning self — a handful of regulars at the counter, the coffee machine doing its soft industrial hiss, the pie case rotating its options with quiet confidence. Ruby herself, who missed nothing, looked up when they came through the door and managed to say "booth in the back, hon" without her face doing anything implicating.

Diane suspected Ruby had been briefed.

They slid into the booth — across from each other, a safe geometry — and Ruby materialized with two mugs and a pot without being asked, which was either extraordinary hospitality or evidence of advance coordination. Probably both.

"Thanks, Ruby," Brian said.

Ruby said nothing, which was louder than anything she could have said.

Diane wrapped both hands around her mug and tried to locate, somewhere in her nervous system, the person she was when she was not terrified. She found her, approximately, and squared her shoulders.

"I want to formally apologize," she said, "for everything that happened at the counter."

"I want to formally tell you that it was the best thing that's happened to me in weeks."

She looked at him. He was not performing sympathy. He meant it.

"That's a very low bar," she said.

"It's been a long winter."

"It really has."

And then they were both smiling, and something recalibrated — the pressure of the thing equalized, became livable, became something she could breathe alongside.

"How long have you been in Ember Creek?" he asked.

"Since November. Four months."

"Where from?"

"Portland."

"Big shift."

"That was — somewhat the point." She said it without apology, which felt like a thing she had been practicing. "I needed a different kind of quiet. Portland quiet and mountain quiet are different."

"They really are." He turned his mug in a slow circle. "I came from Denver. Same impulse, different reason."

She did not ask what the reason was. It was only the first coffee. Some things belonged to later.

"The woodworking — the carpentry," she said instead. "Is that what you did in Denver?"

"Yes. Custom furniture, mostly. Some renovation. Here it's more general — whatever people need."

"Do you like it?"

He looked like the question surprised him slightly, in a good way. Like few people asked him that. "I do. There is something honest about it. You show up, you do the thing, you leave and the thing you made is still there. It doesn't — go away."

She thought about that. "I understand that." And in the back of her mind a sense of ease came over her whole body as she realized what he said, "You show up." What Eddie always said, the kind of man he always strived to be and now, here, in this moment with Brian, he was saying the same thing. Serendipity. Just as she drifted into her thoughts, as she often did, Brian brought her back.

"You work at the bookshop?"

"Part time. I moved here without a solid plan, which is not typical for me." She said this with the self-awareness of someone who had examined this choice from multiple angles. "I thought I'd figure out the rest as I went. Which is — going. Slowly."

"Slowly is fine."

"Says the man who appears to have this town charmed in eight months."

Something moved through his expression. "I don't know about that."

"The town talks," she said. "I've been in the corner listening for four months. You come up."

He looked at her. "What do they say?"

She considered her answer. She was not going to tell him all of it. Not yet. But she could give him something true. "That you show up."

"That's what they say about you too," he said.

She had not expected that. "I've barely been here."

"You walked into the bookshop on your second day. You came to the winter festival. You come into the shop on your days off to sit in the corner and drink tea and—" a small pause "—apparently listen to absolutely everything."

"I was not eavesdropping."

"I know. Linda told me you call it 'community observation.'"

"Linda is generous with information."

"She genuinely is," he agreed, and they were both laughing, and Diane thought: there it is. The loosening. The way a conversation opens when two people have decided, together, to let it.

They stayed for an hour. Ruby refilled their coffees twice and brought pie on the third pass without being asked — the cherry, which Diane had been too nervous to order, and which turned out to be exactly what she needed. They talked about the town, about Susan and her strong opinions about the books Brian brought her. He told her that Susan had cried at one of the novels last fall and made him promise to read it so they could discuss it, and he'd stayed up until midnight to do it, and then they'd talked for two hours and he wasn't sure which of them had been more surprised to discover they had similar taste.

"What kind of books do you like?" Brian asked.

She hesitated. Just a fraction. "I'm getting back into the romances after a long time away from reading."

He did not ask why. He just nodded. "Starting over is better, sometimes. You read something new with fresh eyes."

She thought about the box. About the bookmark two-thirds through. About the ending she had finally read in February with her coffee going cold on the floor.

"Yes," she said. "Exactly."

When they walked out of Ruby's, the late afternoon light was doing something exceptional to the main street — long shadows, gold air, the kind of light that makes an ordinary place look briefly like a painting. They stopped on the sidewalk.

"This was good," Brian said.

"It was." She meant it fully.

"Could we—" he started, and she was fairly sure she held her breath, "—do this again?"

"Yes," she said. "We could do this again."

He smiled. Walked toward his truck. Turned once, briefly.

She walked back toward The Book Nook.

Inside, Linda was behind the counter, Dorothy was inspecting the display she had already inspected six times, and Carla and Beth were in the corner with very straight faces.

Diane came through the door. The bell rang.

"Well?" said Dorothy, abandoning all pretense.

"Back on the clock," said Diane, tying her apron on.

But she was smiling. She knew they could all see it. She let them.

Chapter 13

The Careful Middle

April in the mountains came slow and tentative, as if it were not entirely sure it was welcome yet. Snow still came, but different now — lighter, briefer, apologizing for itself and gone by noon. The trees began their cautious green, just a suggestion of it at the edges, a watercolor underpainting before the real color arrived.

Diane went on four more coffees with Brian in April.

She counted these with the same faithful attention she counted everything, but she had made a private agreement with herself not to attach too much architecture to the counting. They were

coffees. They were pleasant. They were —
something.

The first was on a Thursday, planned this
time, which felt like its own small
development. He texted — she had given
him her number at Ruby's, which had felt
large and then immediately ordinary —
and said he would be in town in the
morning, if she wanted. She said yes
without making herself wait for a suitable
interval first, which was progress.

They sat in the window booth this time
and she told him about Portland. Not all
of it — not yet — but the parts that
belonged to her, the life she had built
there, the work she had been doing
before she decided to stop doing it
(financial analysis, not her love, but
stable). She told him about the city's
particular smell in autumn and how she

loved it. How she had thought she would be there forever.

She did not say: and then something happened and I could not be.

Not yet. There were things that needed their own time.

Brian told her about Denver. About the furniture business, he had started with a friend at twenty-six and sold his share at thirty, not because it was not working but because he had wanted something different for reasons he was still figuring out. About the two years between that and moving here that he called "adjusting," which she understood was its own carefully chosen word.

"What made you pick Ember Creek?" she asked. "Beyond Susan."

He thought about it. "I had visited her every Christmas for twenty years. I always liked how it felt."

"How it felt?"

"Like it was going at the right speed," he said. "Like you could actually catch it."

She thought about the walk down the mountain on her second day, and how the unhurried quality of the town had been the first thing to reach her.

"Yes," she said. "Exactly that."

They were doing that — the exactly that thing. Finding the places where their separate experiences of being alive had arrived at the same point from different directions. It was, Diane found, simultaneously wonderful and terrifying, and she was old enough to know that those two things traveling together usually meant something worth paying attention to.

~

The town was paying attention in its own way.

By April, Brian and Diane were what Linda would describe, to the working group convening over coffee at her kitchen table, as "an ongoing situation with very positive indicators." Dorothy thought they should simply be declared a couple and let the town move on. Carla reminded her that some things needed to arrive at their own pace. Beth said she was simply happy they were both smiling more, which was the only metric that actually mattered, and everyone agreed.

Brian's name came up in Diane's life with regularity she had stopped trying to disguise. She mentioned him to Pete on their weekly calls with what she hoped was casual brevity, and Pete, because he knew her, said nothing but "Mm-hm" in the tone that meant he was quietly delighted.

She mentioned him to herself, at night, which was a different and more honest kind of admission. She lay in the cabin bedroom listening to the pines and had conversations in her head that she would never have in real life — conversations about Eddie, about the way grief worked, about whether the heart was capable of holding more than one great love in it, not sequentially but simultaneously, the first one transformed by loss into something permanent and held, the second one arriving new and tentative and asking if there was room.

Is there room?

There might be room.

She was terrified there was room.

On the third coffee in April, he walked her back toward The Book Nook from Ruby's and they stood outside the green door and it was warm enough that she'd left her coat open, and he was saying something about the Johnson place renovation and how the original floors under the carpet were these wide-plank pine boards that had been hidden for probably fifty years.

"They're extraordinary," he said, with the warmth of someone who loves their work. "This wood — you can see a century in it. Every repair and patch and where the furniture used to stand. It's like — it's the whole life of a house, right there."

She was looking at him while he talked. Not guardedly, not sideways. Just looking.

He noticed. He stopped.

"What?" he said.

"Nothing," she said. "I just—" she tried to find the word and picked the honest one. "I like hearing you talk about things you care about."

He looked at her for a long moment. Something moved through his expression that she did not have a name for yet — something careful and not careful at all.

"Diane," he started.

The green door opened. Dorothy came out with a small bag of books and said, "Oh, Diane, lovely — Linda says your order came in." She clocked the situation with devastating accuracy and added, "I'll leave you both to it," and went down the sidewalk at a pace that was not fast enough to be obvious.

The moment had rearranged itself, as moments did.

"I should go back in," Diane said.

"Yeah." Brian paused. "May I ask you something?"

"Yes."

"Are you — okay? I mean." He was choosing his words. "You don't have to tell me anything. But sometimes you—" another pause "—go somewhere. For a second. And I wondered."

She looked at him for a long moment, gathering her thoughts before speaking.

"I lost someone," she said. "It was two and a half years ago. I'm not—" she found the words she meant "—I'm not broken. I am still putting things back together. Sometimes I go somewhere for a second."

He nodded. Just nodded. No follow-up, no fix, no performance of the right reaction. He just — took it in. Let it be true. "Okay," he said.

"Okay," she said.

"I'll see you Thursday?"

"Thursday," she confirmed.

She went inside. The bell rang.

She stood just inside the door and breathed.

That, she thought, was the careful middle — the place between grief and something else, where you're not sure what the ground is made of yet and you have to test each step but the ground keeps holding, and each time it holds you get a little braver.

She went behind the counter and helped the next customer.

She was, she thought, getting a little braver.

Chapter 14

Susan Henderson Has Thoughts

Susan Henderson requested Diane's company the way she did most things: calmly, specifically, and with the assumption that her company would be accepted, which it would.

"Brian mentioned you," she told Diane on the phone — they had arrived at the phone call stage through a series of small steps that Susan had navigated with considerable strategic skill, primarily involving having Brian mention to Linda that his grandmother loved having company and was somewhat housebound, and Linda relaying this to Diane in a way that made the invitation feel natural. "He mentioned you several times. I thought it was time I met you properly."

Diane arrived on a Saturday in late April with a pot of the lavender shortbread she had been making since she found the recipe in a cookbook at the shop. Susan Henderson was in her armchair by the window with a book open on her lap and the posture of someone who had spent a lifetime making rooms feel like they belonged to her. She was in her seventies, with white hair cut short and sharp blue eyes that were immediately and unmistakably Brian's eyes, or rather, his were hers.

"Sit down," she said, gesturing toward the armchair across from her with the proprietorial ease of a woman who had received company in this room for decades. "Let me look at you."

Diane sat.

"You're prettier than Linda described," Susan said, "which means Linda deliberately undersold you, which means she was being discreet, which is the only thing I reliably trust Linda to be." She reached for one of the shortbreads. "These smell wonderful."

"They're lavender," Diane said. "From a cookbook we have at the shop."

"I know the book. I ordered it for myself two years ago and then decided I was not going to bake anymore because I did not want to be the kind of person who baked at seventy-three and so I did it once and gave the book to Brian to donate. He evidently donated it to the shop." She bit into the shortbread and made a sound of small but real pleasure. "Good. Better than mine were but don't tell me that."

"I absolutely will not."

"Sit forward. Tell me about yourself. Brian has told me the outline, but outlines are insufficient."

Diane found, somewhat to her own surprise, that she wanted to tell her. Susan had the quality of a person who heard things correctly — not just the words but the shape of what was underneath them. She told her about Portland. About the work she had done and why it had stopped meaning something. About the loss — she called it the loss, which felt like the right word for the occasion — and the decision to start over in a mountain town she had heard about from an acquaintance at the worst period of her life and had held onto like a paper crane.

Susan listened to all of it.

"I lost my husband when I was thirty-eight," she said when Diane finished. "Heart attack. He was forty-one. We had two children and a house that had his voice in every room."

Diane did not say anything.

"I stayed," Susan continued. "Because this was where he was, in a way. And then Brian's mother — my daughter — worried I was staying for the wrong reasons, and she was right to worry, and also the reasons were mine and I made peace with them eventually." She looked at Diane steadily. "The question of how long it takes and how much room your heart has is one no one else can answer for you."

"I've been learning that."

"My Brian," Susan said, with the mixture of pride and gentle candor that grandmothers in full command of their faculties deploy, "is a very good man. Not a perfect man. He holds onto things too quietly and sometimes that means he holds onto them until they get heavy, and he should have let them down earlier." She met Diane's eyes. "But when he loves something, he tends it. The way he tends a piece of wood — patiently. Not rushing it. Just bringing out what's already there."

Diane felt something land in her chest. Not heavily. Gently, like a letter through a mail slot.

"I'm not telling you what to do," Susan added. "I am constitutionally incapable of meddling."

Diane, who had by now heard enough of the town's history to know this was the opposite of the truth, said: "Of course not."

Susan smiled. "I like you," she said. "You're subtle. Brian needs subtle. Everyone he has ever been involved with has had a plan and a timeline. You seem like someone who's learned to just be somewhere."

"I'm learning," Diane said.

"That's all being somewhere is."

They had tea. Susan told her about the garden club and the years before her hip, about the roses she had grown on the south fence and her plan to have Brian rebuild the raised bed so she could try again this season. She asked Diane if she gardened and when Diane said not yet,

Susan said "yet" was her favorite word and that there was still time to plant some things if she started soon.

When Diane left, two hours later, Susan pressed her hand at the door and said: "Come again."

"I'd like that," Diane said.

She walked home through the lengthening spring evening thinking about what Susan had said. About tending things. About patience. About rooms that had someone's voice in them.

Her cabin had Eddie's voice in the box in the corner.

But lately, when she came home, she also heard her own voice in it. Her own presence. Her own life, starting to take space.

She thought that was probably what starting over felt like.

Not the old voice going quiet. Just — her own voice getting louder.

Chapter 15
The Spring Fair and the Almost

May arrived in Ember Creek like a long exhale — the snow finally, properly gone, the mountains going green in waves from the valley up, the air carrying something new and warm that made everyone walk a little differently. The Spring Fair was the first outdoor event of the season and the town committed to it with the accumulated enthusiasm of five months of winter.

The fairgrounds were strung with bunting in every color. There were farm animals that the children greeted with the frenzy of people who reunited with old friends. There were food booths and craft tables and a pie competition that Dorothy judged with the focused impartiality of a federal magistrate.

There was a flower-planting station where children could make a pot to take home, which generated a level of concentration in four-year-olds that Diane found genuinely moving.

She went with Carla and Beth, which was becoming the natural shape of things — she was embedded here now, had people, had a context. It still surprised her sometimes, the way the town had made room for her without making a production of it.

She saw Brian near the pie competition at noon, talking to Tom Kettley about something involving roof timbers, based on the hand gestures. He had not seen her yet. She watched him for a moment with the luxury of the unobserved — the effortless way he stood, the way he talked with his hands when he was explaining something technical, the way he listened by going still.

Then Carla said "he's over by the pies" in a tone of utter innocence, and Diane gave her a look, and Carla returned a look of identical innocence.

He saw her when they moved closer. Lifted a hand — she lifted one back. Tom Kettley said something that made Brian smile and he smiled at Tom and then looked back at Diane, and the smile that stayed on his face after that was a different one. A smaller one. Just for her.

She went warm all the way to her toes.

"He's going to say something today," Beth said, with the composure of a woman stating a weather forecast.

"Please stop," Diane said.

"I'm just observing."

"You and I have completely different definitions of 'just.'"

The afternoon was soft and golden. She spent time at the flower booth and came away with a small bouquet of fresh cut flowers that Jo, the candle-maker-turned-fair-volunteer, said, "those are as lovely as you, Diane," which made Diane blush a bit as she continued to walk by. She watched the pie judging, where Dorothy declared the apple-blackberry category winner with a gravitas that suggested the stakes were geopolitical.

And then, late afternoon, she was at the lemonade stand working her way through a cup of something cold and sharp, alone for a moment — Carla had gone to find her daughter, Beth had gone to look at a jewelry booth — when Brian appeared at her left shoulder.

"Hey."

"Hey."

He got a lemonade. They stood there, side by side, looking at the fair.

"Good day," he said.

"Really good."

A comfortable beat of quiet. She had noticed they had comfortable quiet now — it was not effortful or charged, just ordinary silence. It was nice.

"I want to show you something," he said. "If you have time. The Johnson place — the floors. I told you about them."

She had thought about those floors. About a century in the wood.

"Yes," she said. "I'd like to see that."

They walked from the fairgrounds to the Johnson place, which was about a mile up the road. As they started their walk, the road from the fairgrounds opened up almost immediately into a wide stretch of open prairie, the kind of path that made you feel small in the best possible way — tall grass on either side swaying in the easy mountain breeze, the sky enormous overhead, the noise of the fair dissolving behind them until there was nothing left but the sound of their footsteps and the birds singing. It was the kind of quiet that felt earned. Diane had the small bouquet of fresh cut flowers she'd picked up tucked against her side — yellow and white and something purple she didn't know the name of — and she was thinking about where she would put them in the cabin when Brian glanced over.

"Fresh flowers?" he asked.

"I bought them for the cabin," she said. "To brighten it up a little."

He nodded slowly, "You know — you deserve to have someone buying those for you."

She felt the warmth hit her face before she had any say in the matter. She looked down at the bouquet, then at the path ahead, then at absolutely nothing in particular. She cleared her throat, "Oh — is that a meadowlark? I think I hear a — "

"Oh no you don't!" There was a smile in his voice, low and certain. "I know exactly what you're doing. I mean it, Diane. Someone should be buying those flowers for you."

She looked at him at that moment, unable to help it, and found him already looking back at her with that steady, unhurried expression that she had never once successfully deflected. She opened her mouth. Closed it. The meadowlark, wherever it was, offered nothing useful.

Brian lifted his chin toward the tree line ahead. "There she is," he said simply. "The Johnson place."

Diane turned to look — the long white farmhouse coming into view through the tall grass, patient and waiting — and she exhaled slowly, grateful for the rescue but then again, not entirely sure she was.

He unlocked the front door, and she stepped in and he took her through to the main room, where the old carpet had been rolled back and the floors lay open in the afternoon light.

They were extraordinary.

Wide pine boards, darkened with age and use, with the warmth of old wood that has lived with people for generations. She could see the patches he had described — the places where a repair had been made twenty years ago or forty years ago, different wood but the same intention. The places where furniture had stood for so long the floor remembered it. The whole life of a house.

"Oh," she said.

"Yeah," he agreed quietly.

She walked across them slowly. They sounded different under her feet than new floors — a deeper sound, a more considered one. She stopped near the window where the light came through and crouched down to look more closely at the grain.

Brian crouched down next to her.

They were close. The kind of close that has its own gravity.

"The way you talk about the wood," she said, not looking up, "is the way I feel about a really good book. Like something's alive in it that you didn't put there."

"Exactly," he said.

She looked up. He was already looking at her.

Close. The afternoon light. The old house, patient and open around them.

"Diane."

Her name in his voice, at this distance, landed somewhere deep in her body that made her heart race and her body yearn for something she had forgotten she desired.

"Brian."

He looked at her like he was preparing to share something that made him nervous but excited all at once. His body leaned towards hers and the physical tension between them caused Diane to take a sudden breath in. In that breath Diane smelt the warm cedar and pine smell of Brian mixed with the old panels of wood in the Johnson house.

Diane's heart continued to race, as anticipation and desire all blended into a charge almost unbearable within her skin until the taunting silence ended when Brian spoke.

"I would very much like to—" he started.

His phone rang.

He closed his eyes and breathed heavier as he reached for his phone.

"I'm sorry." He pulled it out. "It's Susan. I have to—"

"Go," Diane said. "Go."

He answered as he stood, and she heard Susan's voice on the phone saying something about the pharmacy closing at five and him needing to pick something up. He was moving toward the door, one hand raised in apology, and she waved him on and stayed on the floor for a moment longer, looking at the old boards.

A century in the wood.

She pressed her hand flat against the floor.

She thought: be patient. It is almost there.

She got up and drove home through the new May evening and sat on her porch with the lavender seedling on the railing and the mountain ahead of her, and she said, to no one and to the only person it made sense to say it too:

"Eddie. I think I am ready. I think — I think something is starting. Is this okay?"

The pines moved in the evening wind. The mountains were enormous and still.

> *Tell me the best version of the story, Di.*

She pressed her hand to her chest.

"I'm trying," she said. "I'm really trying."

Chapter 16

The Thing About Rain

It rained for four days in a row in late May, which in a mountain town means something different than city rain — heavier, more committed, the kind of rain that doesn't perform but simply falls with purpose, intent, and an invitation to stay indoors and become a different version of yourself.

Diane accepted the invitation.

She read. She read three books in four days, which was more than she'd read in any four-day stretch in two and a half years, and each one felt like stretching a muscle that had been held still too long — a little painful at first, then increasingly fluid, then something like joy.

She called Pete on the second rainy day. He was at school; she left a voicemail. "I read two books in two days, and I just wanted someone to know." She paused. "That's all. That is the whole call. Bye."

He called back within forty minutes: "Diane," he said. "That's everything. That's the whole thing."

She cried a little. This was not her returning to who she was, this was her becoming the best version of her story now. She was getting better at letting herself be present, be joyful and find excitement for the future.

On the third rainy day, Brian texted: "Stuck inside. Susan is convinced she can beat me at rummy and she is right. You surviving the rain?"

She smiled at her phone for a long time before responding. "Surviving excellently. Tell Susan I said rummy is a game of skill and she should absolutely win."

"She is reading this over my shoulder and she says thank you."

"She's reading over your shoulder?"

"She's been reading over my shoulder for thirty years. I've stopped noticing."

Diane laughed. Typed: "What's Susan reading these days?"

"Just finished one she called 'magnificent and also infuriating, which is the mark of a truly great love story.' I'm taking her word for it."

"Have you read it?"

Brian paused.

"...She might have made me read the last two chapters."

"And?"

Another pause.

"It was a very good last two chapters."

Diane put the phone down and stared at the ceiling and felt something in her chest do a quiet, involuntary thing that she recognized as happiness. Not the large obvious kind. The small, specific, entirely real kind that lives in ordinary moments and is only visible if you are paying attention.

On the fourth rainy day, a knock on her door.

This was unexpected. She was in her reading sweater — an enormous, shapeless thing in a color she called "worn burgundy" and which Pete called "what is that"— with her hair up, a book open on her lap and the fire going. She was not prepared for visitors. She went to the door, opened it and Brian was on her porch with rain on his jacket, his hair wet and a paper bag from the bakery.

"Hi," he said.

"Hi," she said.

"Susan sent croissants. She said the rain called for croissants. I was already in the car." Brian paused, "I could — if you're busy—"

"Come in," she said.

He came in. He looked at the cabin — the bookshelves she had built out carefully over months, the fire, the open book, the life of a person who had moved here and stayed and made it theirs.

"Nice," he said simply. She understood he meant it fully.

They ate croissants by the fire, and she made tea because it was that kind of afternoon and he did not tease her about the tea, just accepted the mug. He told her about the Johnson place, which was coming together now, the floors refinished and glowing. She told him about the books she had been reading. He asked questions about them, real ones, the kind that made her realize he was listening to understand and not just to respond.

It went quiet at some point in the easy, unselfconscious way of rainy afternoons.

"Can I ask you something?" she said.

"Yeah."

"The Johnson place floors. You said you could see the whole life of the house in them. What do you do with a floor like that? Do you restore it to what it was, or do you — accept that it has been through things?"

He thought about what Diane asked carefully. "Both. You clean it up. You repair what is damaged. But you do not pretend the years did not happen. You finish it in a way that respects what it's been through."

She looked at the fire as she listened to Brian's answer. It was an answer that could not have been more perfect if they had planned it. It was honest and the exact answer Diane had hoped to hear without truly knowing what she wanted from that question until after Brian answered.

Unprovoked, Diane shared:

"I lost my boyfriend," she said. "Two and a half years ago. His name was Eddie. He was — he was my person. And I moved here because I needed somewhere that did not know that version of me. Somewhere I could figure out who I was after."

Brian said nothing. He was listening with his whole body.

"I'm telling you that because I think you should know it," she said. "I'm not — I'm not in the middle of it the way I was. But it is part of me. It doesn't go away."

"I know," he said. "It shouldn't."

She looked at him. "You're not scared of it?"

"Why would I be scared of the fact that you loved someone?" He said it plainly, like it was the obvious answer to an easy question. "That's not a warning. That's just — who you are."

She had not, she realized, expected that. She had prepared herself for the version where she said it and he became careful, or changed the subject, or offered the platitudes that well-meaning people deployed because they did not know what else to do.

He did none of those things. He just — sat with it. With her.

"Okay," she said.

"Okay," he said.

They sat by the fire until the rain eased. When he left, he stopped at the door and turned back, and she thought: here it is, and her heart did its particular thing.

"Thursday?" he said.

"Thursday," she confirmed.

He left. She stood in the open doorway for a minute and listened to the rain dripping from the eaves of her porch and thought: well, that was not it, it was more.

Chapter 17

The Town Holds Its Breath

By June, the town of Ember Creek had developed, on the subject of Diane Calloway and Brian Henderson, something approaching a collective emotional investment.

This had happened gradually and then all at once, in the way of most things in small places — a small observation here, a corroborating detail there, the accumulation of sightings and reports until the whole became more than its parts and suddenly there was a story, and the story was the town's favorite thing to have.

Linda's working group had expanded, somewhat organically, to include Ruby, Jo the candle maker, Henry Baker who was eighty-one and had nothing but time and opinions, and Cal, who had bought the mystery novel for his wife on Valentine's Day and had been coming into the shop weekly since and was now, as Linda privately noted, one of the best-read people in town. He had also developed strong feelings about Brian and Diane.

"They were at the Spring Fair," he reported at one of the working group's informal gatherings at Ruby's. "I watched them walk to the Johnson place together. She came back alone but she was smiling the whole way to her car. The whole walk!"

This was received with the warm gravity of significant intelligence.

"Something happened at the Johnson place," Dorothy said.

"Or almost happened," Linda corrected. "Susan called him about the pharmacy."

A collective sound.

"The pharmacy," Dorothy said.

"It's close," Linda said. "It's very close. Patience."

They had patience. They had made considerable investment. They channeled their energy into the form of gentle, uncoordinated, entirely plausible deniable support of both parties at every opportunity — a word here, a knowing smile there, the careful engineering of proximity and occasion.

None of which they admitted to, because they were all excellent people who deeply respected the autonomy and privacy of the individuals involved.

They also really, really wanted them to get together.

~

June brought the Summer Kick-off potluck to Tom Kettley's farm, which Diane attended in a yellow dress she had bought in the city and had never worn until now.

She saw Brian when she came through the gate. He saw her at the same moment. Brian maintained eye contact with Diane as he crossed the field to reach her.

"Hi," he said.

"Hi."

He looked at the dress. Back at her face. "You look—" a pause, and something in his eyes she had been learning to read "—beautiful."

"Thank you." She blushed and felt warm in a way that had nothing to do with the June evening. "I've had this dress for two years and never worn it."

"Why not?"

"The occasion wasn't right." She met his eyes. "Now it is."

Something shifted. The small careful space between them, which had been maintained with considerable mutual effort over months, did something it had never quite done before — it pressed in, became thinner.

"I've been wanting to say something to you," he said.

She waited.

"I—" he started, and then Tom Kettley appeared with a tray of something grilled and a massive smile and said, "Brian! Diane! Perfect, come eat, we have been waiting—" and took them both by the arm and steered them toward the tables, because Tom Kettley was a man of great hospitality and absolutely terrible timing.

Diane caught Brian's eye over Tom's shoulder. He made a face — a small, helpless, funny face — and she laughed.

Later, near the fire, she found herself standing next to him as the party settled into its final hours. The sky above the field was enormous and filled with stars. Someone nearby was playing guitar, something slow and easy.

"Tomorrow," Brian said. Low, just for her.

She looked up at him. "Tomorrow?"

"Whatever I was going to say. Tomorrow."

"Okay," she said.

"I'm not — I just don't want to do it at a potluck."

"That's fair."

"I'm going to tell you, Diane."

"I know," she said. And she did. She was entirely ready. "I know you are."

They stood in the starlight and she thought: this is the story. This is what it feels like when a story is about to turn a corner.

Chapter 18

Tomorrow

He called at eight in the morning, and she answered on the second ring.

She had been awake since before light — not from anxiety, not from the restless, circular thinking that had kept her up so many nights in the two years before this one. This was something different. She had woken alert, her whole body quietly awake, like it already knew something the rest of her was still catching up to. She had laid still for a few minutes, listening to the pines, listening to her own breathing, and then she had gotten up and pulled on her boots and her jacket and gone out into the mountain morning before it had fully decided what it wanted to be.

The air was cold and clean in the way it was only at this elevation, at this hour — thin and sharp and carrying the smell of pine resin and damp earth. Something that was just the mountain itself, present and enormous and entirely indifferent to the smallness of any individual life. She had loved that about it from the very first morning she had walked this trail. The mountain did not need anything from her. It did not ask her how she was doing. It simply held her, without effort and without judgment.

Her phone buzzed in her jacket pocket.

Brian.

"Are you on the trail?" he asked. His voice was morning-rough.

"Yes," she said.

"May I come join you?"

"Yes, I would like that" she said.

He met her at the trailhead eighteen minutes later, which meant he had been dressed already, which meant he had been awake already, which meant she was not the only one who had woken up this morning sensing something in the air.

He was in his work clothes — dark canvas pants, the navy flannel she had seen him wear a dozen times, the collar open against the early chill. He was carrying coffee in each hand, his hair was doing the thing it did, and he looked exactly like himself, which was the thing she had come to love most about him. There was no performance in him, no arrangement. He was just — there. Warm and solid and already smiling at her before she even said a word.

She fell into step beside him.

They walked into the pines without speaking and the silence between them was the comfortable kind, the kind that had been earned over four months of Thursday coffees, snowed-in afternoons, six events, seven near-misses and one rainy day when he'd shown up at her door with Susan's croissants and stayed by her fire until the world outside had quieted. The silence of two people who had already learned each other well enough to know that not every moment required filling.

The trail climbed. The trees thinned. Below them, the valley was still holding the last of the morning mist — long pale ribbons of it threading between the tree lines, the rooftops of Ember Creek just visible at the valley floor.

Their town, Ember Creek.

Theirs, in a way she was only just beginning to understand.

At the ridge, where the trees opened completely and the view reached all the way to the far range of mountains still holding their snow, Brian stopped walking.

Diane stopped beside him.

He stood for a moment looking at the valley. She looked at the valley too — at the mist burning slowly off as the morning warmed, at the way the light was starting to reach the mountain faces to the east and turn them from grey to gold.

"I've been trying to find the right way to say this for a while," he said.

"You don't have to say anything the *right way.*"

He was quiet for a moment. She could feel him gathering it — carefully, like a man who had learned the hard way that words said carelessly could not be unsaid.

"I've been here eight months," he said. "And I've been okay. That is the honest word for it — okay. I like this town and the work and taking care of Susan and I do not regret a single day of it. But then you came here." He stopped.

Took a deep breath in.

"And I started being more than okay. And I have been trying to be patient about it. Trying not to push on something before it, you, were ready."

She kept her eyes on the valley. She could feel the warmth of him beside her — not touching, not yet, just the warmth that a person carries, the warmth that you only notice when you have spent enough time near them that their presence has become something your body recognizes.

"Because I told you I was still putting things back together," she said.

"Yes." He turned to look at her. "But I think you've been putting things back together for a while now, Diane. I think you're not as close to the beginning of it as you were when you got here."

She looked at the valley. The mist was almost gone from the lower reaches. The morning was opening.

"No," she said. "I'm not."

"So." He breathed. She heard it — the single breath he took to settle himself, the way she had seen him take a breath before he picked up a tool he needed to use carefully. "I would like to tell you how I feel. If that's all right."

She turned to face him.

"It's all right," she said.

He looked at her for a long moment. Really looked — the way he looked at things he was working with, the way he had looked at the floors of the Johnson place, reading the grain, learning what was there before deciding what to do with it. His eyes were very blue in the morning light. She had thought about his eyes more times than she could account for, and standing here, four feet away, with the mountain open behind him, she thought that she had never quite done them justice in her own mind. They were the kind of blue that changed with the light — darker in the evening, lighter now, the precise color of the sky just before it committed fully to morning.

"I think about you all the time," he said. Simply. No preamble, no softening — just the plain truth of it, set down between them. "I think about the way you listen to things, like you're cataloguing them, storing them away. I think about how you got good at this town's gossip faster than anyone Linda can remember, which I genuinely think says everything important about who you are. I think about the way you talk about books — like they're places you've actually lived in, not just read about."

She was smiling.

"I think about you coming around the corner of a hat booth at a January market," he said, "and making me lose my train of thought so completely that I had to stand there for a full minute just pretending to look at hats." A small, rueful sound escaped him. "I've been losing it fairly regularly ever since."

She laughed — a real one, startled out of her. And the laughing made something loosen in her chest, some last thing she had not known she was still holding.

"I know you loved someone," he said, and his voice was gentler now, careful the way hands are careful with something valuable. "I know that doesn't go away and I'm not asking you to pretend it does. I am not asking you to give me what you gave him. I am just—" He paused. Found what he wanted to say. "I'm asking if there's room. For me?"

The valley below them was waking up. Somewhere behind her, the bird with its three descending notes was doing the thing it did — three notes, a pause, three notes again, like a question that kept asking itself.

She looked at Brian.

She thought about four months ago — about the moving truck and the cold gas station coffee and the single earbud and the playlist she had titled with an optimism she had not yet earned. She thought about the box in the corner of her cabin, about Eddie's handwriting on the side of it, the small careful heart drawn underneath. She thought about the six minutes she had given herself to cry on the first night, the timer she had set as a promise that grief had an edge even when it did not feel like it. She thought about all the ways she had tried to be brave and small at the same time — brave enough to come here, small enough to stay in the corner of The Book Nook with her tea and her pretend notepad, watching the town from a safe distance.

She thought about Eddie.

She let herself think about him fully, the way she had learned to — not as an intrusion, not as something to manage or contain, but as a presence. The warm, specific, irreplaceable presence of a person she had loved completely and lost completely and would carry completely for the rest of her life.

Tell me the best version of the story, Di.

She pressed her hand to her chest, briefly. Just for a second. A greeting and a goodbye at once.

Then she looked at Brian.

"I've been scared," she said. Her voice was shaky. "Not of you. Of what it means — to want this again. To discover that part of me is still alive and functional and completely capable of—" She stopped. Tried again. "I thought it was broken. After Eddie. I thought the part of me that could want this, that could believe in it, was just — gone. And then I moved here. And you kept showing up."

Something moved across his face. Something that was not quite a smile — something more serious than that, more careful, like a man receiving news he had been hoping for and had not let himself believe in yet.

"And I realized," she said, "that it wasn't gone. It was just waiting. Waiting until I was somewhere safe enough to feel it again." She looked at him — at the blue eyes and the morning light and the way he was standing completely still. "This town is safe. You are safe. And I don't want to keep standing on the edge of something I actually want and calling it caution."

"Diane."

Her name in his voice, at this proximity, with the mountain behind him and the morning wide open around them — it landed in her chest like the first note of a song she had forgotten she knew.

"There's room," she said as her voice broke and tears flooded her eyes. "There is absolutely room, Brian."

He closed the distance between them.

Quickly. With the urgency of someone afraid that the moment would vanish if he did not move fast enough. He closed it the way he did most things — deliberately, with his whole attention, like a man who had decided something and was not going to be careless about it. He raised one hand and placed it against the side of her face, his palm warm against her cheek, his thumb tracing a line just below her cheekbone so gently it barely qualified as touch at all — just the suggestion of it, a question in the pressure of his fingertips.

She turned into it. Her face tilted toward his hand the way a plant tilts toward a window, not because it decided to but because some things are simply instinct.

She heard him exhaling and as she closed her eyes to allow the tears to escape her eyes, he kissed her.

It was not soft, the way first kisses in stories sometimes are — tentative and half-formed, as though both people are still deciding. This was not a question. This was an answer. Months of questions and almosts and near-misses and careful distances, and now — this. His mouth on hers with a certainty that made her breath leave her completely, both hands coming up to cup her face like she was something he'd been afraid of dropping, and she felt the warmth of him — all of it, the warmth she'd been sitting near for months at coffee counters and fairgrounds and in front of her own fireplace — pouring into her like light through a window that had been shut a very long time.

Her hands found the front of his flannel and she held on.

She had not been held in two and a half years. She had not let herself want to be held. And now, here, with the mountain holding steady behind them and the morning breaking fully open, she understood the difference between surviving and living in a way that no amount of quiet cabin days and chamomile tea and careful, patient grieving had quite managed to teach her. This was the difference. This — warmth of being wanted by a specific person, of being known and still chosen, of coming home to something you did not know you had been looking for.

She kissed him with everything she had.

With the four months of almost, the seven near-misses, the rainy afternoon by the fire, the Johnson place floors and the box she'd finally opened in February and the books that still had Eddie's handwriting in the margins and the bird with its three notes and the morning walks and the chamomile tea and all the ways this town had held her when she didn't know she needed holding. All of it. She put all of it into kissing Brian Henderson on a ridge at eight thousand feet on a June morning with the whole valley below them and the whole future ahead.

She finally knew the answer.

~

When they finally broke apart, neither of them moved.

He did not step back. She leaned in. The hands that had been holding her face slid down — one settling at her jaw, one finding the small of her back — and she stayed exactly where she was, her forehead tipped forward until it rested against his chest, her hands still holding the front of his flannel, and they stood like that in the cool mountain morning and breathed.

His breath was unsteady. She was glad that she was not the only one undone.

"Okay," she whispered, when she finally could, still halfway out of breath.

The word came out soft and shaky and she meant it more completely than she had ever meant a single syllable in her life.

He laughed — quietly, just a breath of it warm against her forehead. "Okay," he agreed.

She felt his arms wrap around her then, both arms coming around her and drawing her in against his chest, and she let herself go there. Let herself stop holding herself upright by her own effort and just — leaned in. Into the warmth of him. Into the steady, certain solidity of a man who showed up when he said he was going to and built things that lasted.

She fit.

That was the thing she had not expected and that she felt most clearly in that moment — she fit. Not perfectly in the way of things that have not been worn yet, but perfectly in the way of a key that was made for a specific lock, where the fit is so right it feels like recognition rather than discovery. Her head against his chest. His chin coming to rest on top of her head. His heartbeat under her ear — steady, a little fast, honest.

She closed her eyes.

Above them, the sky was fully committed to morning now, the light warm and golden on the high mountain faces and spreading slowly down into the valley. Below them, Ember Creek was waking.

~

Brian held her.

He held her and he thought about nothing useful at all, which was unusual for him. He was, by nature, a person whose mind ran ahead — planning the next task, the next repair, the next thing that needed doing. Even at rest, some part of him was always cataloguing. But not now. Now his mind had gone quiet in the specific, profound way it only went quiet when he was working with his hands — that deep absorption where time stopped being a line you were moving along and became a pool you were standing in.

He was standing in it now with Diane.

He was aware of the weight of her against him — not heavy, just present. He was aware of the way she had come into his arms fully, the way she had simply let herself arrive there, as though she had made the decision before her body had and the body was just catching up. He basked in the smell of her hair — vanilla and cold mountain air and something faintly floral that he recognized as the hand cream she kept at the counter at The Book Nook.

He thought: I should have said hello sooner.

The thought arrived with a small, private ache — not regret exactly, more the bittersweet recognition that had come with every near-miss, every festival, market, and potluck where they had been within arm's reach of each other and had not closed it. All those months of careful distance, of patience that had felt like the right thing but that now, with her actually in his arms, felt like time he had not understood the value of until it was spent.

He should have said hello a hundred times before Linda arranged the one that finally counted.

He pressed his lips to the top of her head. Just lightly. Just enough.

He felt her exhaling.

The way she fit against him — it was the thing that kept arriving in his mind and displacing everything else. He was not a man who reached easily for poetic language, but there was no other word for it: she fit. The specific angle of her head against his chest. The way her hands, which had been gripping the front of his flannel during the kiss, had slowly relaxed and were now lying flat against him, open-palmed, as though she had stopped bracing and was simply resting. The way he could feel her breathing — the small, regular rise and fall of it — and how his own breathing had adjusted without his telling it too, slowing to match hers, the two of them finding the same rhythm without trying.

Like she had always been meant to be there.

Like he had always been meant to be the one holding her.

He did not know how long they stood like that.

Long enough for both of them to understand that this was not an ending.

This was the part where something started.

~

Diane was thinking about Eddie.

He would have liked this, she thought. He would have wanted this for me.

She pressed her cheek more firmly against Brian's chest. Felt his arms tighten slightly in response — just a fraction, just enough to tell her he had noticed.

The grief was still there. She knew it would always be there, some version of it — a permanent weather system in some quieter region of her chest. She had made her peace with that. She had stopped wanting to be the person who was over it and had started becoming, instead, the person who carried it with grace.

But there was something else here now. Something that had been growing quietly. Growing toward whatever warmth was available.

Brian.

Brian was warm and he had looked at her — really looked, the way people rarely do — and had not been frightened by what he saw there. The loss. The careful reconstruction. The woman who still sometimes went somewhere for a second and came back quieter. He had seen all of it and had asked: is there room?

There was room.

She tilted her head back to look at him. He was already looking down at her — she had felt the shift of his attention before she had moved, some awareness of her lifting her face toward his.

"Hi," she said.

It was a ridiculous thing to say but, she said it anyway.

His mouth curved. That small, specific smile that was just for her.

"Hi," he said back.

Gazing into each other's eyes, neither of them moved.

Below them, Ember Creek went about its morning. The mist was completely gone from the valley now. The day was open and entirely certain of itself.

She laid her cheek back against his chest.

Brian held her.

The mountain held them both.

~

They walked back down the mountain through the full warmth of mid-morning and through the pines unbothered by the fact that everything was different now.

At some point, between one step and the next, his hand found hers.

She held it.

She thought about the warmth of his hand and the sound of their boots on the trail and the way the light came through the branches at angles that made everything look as though it had been painted rather than grown.

The trail leveled out. The cabin came into view through the trees.

Brian walked her to the door.

He stopped on the porch and looked at her for a long moment, the same way he had looked at her on the ridge, with his full and unhurried attention.

"Thursday?" he said.

She laughed. Because Thursday was their thing — their coffee, their counter at Ruby's, their reliable and unglamorous and completely wonderful Thursday — and the fact that it still existed, that it was still the word that meant them, felt right in a way she couldn't have explained but didn't need to.

"Thursday," she confirmed.

He leaned forward and kissed her once more — soft this time, brief, just a press of his mouth against hers that said: this is real, I am not going anywhere, I will see you Thursday.

Then he walked back down the mountain road to his truck.

She stood on the porch and watched him go.

The morning was entirely golden now. Her lavender was purple and fragrant and full of small bees doing their small bee business, completely unimpressed by the significance of the morning.

She pressed the back of her hand to her lips.

She stood there for a long time, in the warmth, in the morning, in the life that she had come here to build and that was — she understood now, fully, without reservation — being built.

> *Tell me the best version of the story, Di.*

She smiled at the mountain.

She was living in it.

Chapter 19

The Town Finds Out

It took four hours for the information to complete its circuit through Ember Creek, which was, by the town's standards, a measured and dignified pace.

Susan found out first, because Brian called her every morning and this morning was no different except that his voice had a quality in it, she had not heard in several years. She recognized it the way you recognize something you have been waiting for — not with surprise but with the deep, settled satisfaction of a woman whose patience had been entirely vindicated. She said "I see" in a tone that communicated approximately forty words of knowing subtext and when she hung up the phone she sat for a long moment in her armchair by the window and looked at the bird feeder and felt her eyes fill, briefly, with tears that belong not to sadness but to relief.

Then she called Linda.

Linda received the information with the composed satisfaction of a woman whose long-term investment had just paid every dividend she had anticipated plus several she had not. She set the phone down carefully. She went to the back room. She came back with a small vase — white ceramic, a sprig of lavender in it — and placed it on the counter of The Book Nook without explanation, because none was needed. Dorothy arrived for her Tuesday visit, looked at the vase, looked at Linda, and said: "Well."

"Well," Linda agreed.

Carla found out from her mother. Beth already knew because Ruby had called her, and Ruby had gotten it from Henry Baker, who had gotten it from Tom Kettley, who had seen Brian's truck on the mountain road at eight in the morning and had drawn a conclusion that turned out to be correct. Cal came into the shop at eleven and found Linda with the lavender vase and the expression and said "finally!" with such feeling that Dorothy looked up from her book and nodded once, slowly, in complete agreement.

By noon, Ember Creek had reached its consensus. It expressed this consensus the way it expressed most things — with warmth and without ceremony, in the ordinary continuation of its daily life that somehow felt, today, lit from a slightly different angle.

~

Diane came in for her Tuesday afternoon shift not knowing any of this.

She arrived — a softness at the edges of her, a quality of uncollected happiness that she had not quite organized into anything yet. She hung up her jacket, she tied her apron, and she made her tea.

Linda said, "Good afternoon, Diane," in the tone of a woman who knew everything.

Diane looked at the vase. At Linda. "How?"

"Susan is very efficient."

Diane looked puzzled as she stared at Linda.

"He called his grandmother from the trail."

"He calls her every morning. Anything else would have been suspicious."

Dorothy, from her chair, without looking up from her book: "We are very happy for you, Diane."

Carla arrived through the door at that exact moment with the energy of a woman who had been texting for the last hour trying to determine if she could drop by the shop on a Tuesday afternoon without it seeming contrived. She came directly to the counter and put her arms around Diane for longer than the occasion technically required. "We love you," she said into Diane's shoulder. "We love this. We have all been losing our collective minds for months."

"How many people—" Diane started.

"The number," Linda said gently, "is not the point. The point is that this town loves you and it loves Brian and it has been holding its breath since approximately the second week of December."

Diane looked around the shop. At Linda and the lavender. At Dorothy in her chair with her book and her quietly satisfied expression. At Carla, who was still slightly pink around the eyes when something makes them glad.

Something opened in her chest. Not surprise — she had known, on some level, for months, that the town was watching. That it had taken the two of them into its warm, communal regard and decided they were worth paying attention to. But knowing it abstractly and feeling it like this, right now, was different.

"This town," she said. She meant it as more than two words.

"This town," Linda agreed. And there was pride in her voice that was not about the town in general, but about what the town had quietly, deliberately, chosen to do for two people who needed it.

Dorothy looked up. "In thirty-one years of living here, I don't believe I've enjoyed anything quite so thoroughly as watching the two of you nearly speak to each other at six consecutive community events."

"Dorothy!"

"I stand by my enjoyment of it entirely."

Carla said: "The fence gap at the Maple Sugar Festival. That was my moment. That was when I knew."

Beth, appearing from somewhere near the back shelves with the serene timing of a woman who had been waiting patiently for her cue: "The orange hat. For me it was the orange hat."

Diane pressed both palms flat onto the counter. "I wear that hat."

"We know," said Dorothy.

~

Brian came in that afternoon.

The bell rang — ding ding — and Diane looked up from the counter as the woman who had just kissed this man on a ridge that morning, which rearranged how she stood and what her face did without any consultation with the rest of her.

He came through the green door in his work clothes. He crossed to the counter directly, and he stood right in front of her, and for a moment neither of them said anything — just looked at each other.

"Hi," he said.

"Hi," she said.

He looked around the shop, which had acquired, in the last two hours, an unusual density of regulars who were all very conspicuously engaged with other things. "The whole town knows." Diane shared in a whisper.

"Very quickly."

"Are you okay with that?" he whispered back.

She thought about Linda's lavender and Carla's arms around her shoulders and Dorothy's thirty-one years of thoroughly enjoying small-town living. She thought about the way this community had made room for her from the very first Tuesday she had walked through the green door with chilly air on her coat and no plan at all.

"Yes," she said. "Completely okay with that."

He reached across the counter and tucked a strand of hair behind her ear — such a small gesture, so simple, and it undid her completely. His fingers barely grazed her cheek, and she felt it all through her body.

From the back corner, Carla made a sound she immediately converted into a cough that disrupted Diane's thoughts of Brian.

"Dinner tonight?" Brian asked. His voice was low, just for her. "I'll cook."

"You cook?"

"Susan has been teaching me. Under considerable protest regarding my technique, which she has described as 'enthusiastic but misguided."

"High praise."

"It's the best I've gotten out of her." The corner of his mouth lifted. "Come to dinner. I can't promise it'll be perfect."

She thought: I do not need it to be perfect. I have had enough of waiting for perfect.

"I'll come," she said.

He held the door for the customer behind him and left, and the bell rang twice on his way out — ding ding.

Linda appeared at her shoulder. "Well."

"Please," Diane said.

"I'm simply observing."

"You are incapable of simply observing."

"That," Linda said contentedly, "is entirely possible."

~

The evening came and Diane was excited to get ready for dinner.

She stood in front of her closet for twenty minutes until she settled on a soft green linen dress she'd bought in Portland and barely worn, it was the color of new pine growth, the color of early spring, the color of things beginning — and a cardigan because the June evenings still had a bite to them up here, and her good boots, and the small gold earrings that had belonged to her mother.

She drove down the mountain road to town with the windows down.

The evening was extraordinary in the way that June evenings in the mountains sometimes were — long and gold and so clear it felt like the air had been washed, everything precise and illuminated and offering itself to be seen. She passed the trailhead where they had walked that morning and felt the memory of it like warmth between her ribs. She passed the turnoff to The Book Nook and thought of Linda's lavender. She drove the last half mile to the small house on Alder Street where Brian lived — she had never been inside it, had only ever seen it from the road — she parked and sat for a moment with the engine off.

She was nervous.

She had not been nervous in an exceedingly long time. Grief had taken a lot of things from her and nervousness was one of them — it was hard to be nervous about small things when you had survived large ones. But this was a different kind of nervousness. Not fear. Not the dread she had learned to carry like a stone in her pocket for two years. This was the lighter, fizzing, almost-pleasant nervousness of anticipation. Of wanting something and being close to having it.

~

His house was small and honest, the way things in Ember Creek tended to be — a one-story house on a quiet street with a front porch that held two chairs and a stack of lumber that had not made it to wherever it was going yet. The lights inside were warm and low. Through the kitchen window she could see him moving, and for a moment she stood on the front walk and just watched — Brian Henderson in his own kitchen, sleeves rolled to the elbows, doing something to a pot on the stove with the focused attention he brought to everything.

She had the strangest, most specific feeling of recognition. As though she had stood here before. As though this was a window she had always known she would look through eventually.

After a few minutes of getting lost in her own thoughts, Diane walked up to Brian's door and knocked.

He opened the door and the smell of garlic, olive oil and something herbed came out to meet her and behind it, the warm smell of his house — wood, linseed oil and the faint sweetness of sawdust that clung to the spaces he occupied — and she stepped inside and it felt like stepping into somewhere she had been before.

"You came," he said.

"You asked."

He looked at her — at the green dress and the gold earrings— with an expression that was quiet and made her feel, for the second time that day, entirely seen.

"You look—" He stopped. Let out a deep breath. "You're Beautiful, Diane."

"Thank you," she said. And then, because she was Diane and she could not help it: "Susan was right about your cooking instincts — something's boiling over."

He spun back to the stove with a sound of mild alarm that made her laugh all the way into the kitchen.

~

The kitchen was small, warm, and smelled wonderful despite the close call with the sauce. The pasta was a wide, flat noodle with a sauce of roasted tomatoes, garlic, and fresh herbs from the small pot on his windowsill — basil and thyme and what he called "whatever Susan said to add next, I stopped questioning her." There was bread, slightly overdone at the edges, which he presented with the frank disclaimer that the oven ran hot, and he had not fully made peace with it yet. There was wine poured into mismatched glasses, which he pointed out immediately and made her love the evening before it started.

The table in the kitchen was small — the kind that fit two people and nothing extra, where your knees were almost touching. The light above it was warm and low. Outside the window, the long June evening was still holding its gold.

Diane stuck her fork into the pasta, spinning it on to the fork and took a bite.

"Well?" he eagerly asked.

"Brian."

"Be honest."

"This is genuinely good." Diane said with a warm smile on her face as she finished chewing the bite of pasta she just took.

He exhaled. "Susan said the same thing, but she was very complimentary about it in a way that I found suspicious."

"Susan doesn't do false comfort. I've spent enough time with her to know that."

"That's true." He picked up his fork. "She told me last week that my mashed potatoes were 'adequate,' and I could tell it cost her."

Diane laughed — the kind of laugh that arrived without warning and left her leaning slightly forward over the table. He was looking at her when she straightened, with that expression he got sometimes: surprised and warm and like he was memorizing something.

"What?" she said.

"Nothing." He turned back to his plate. "I just—" A pause. "I like the way you laugh."

She looked at her pasta. Felt warmth move across her face. "You like my laugh?"

"Yes. I have been noticing it since December. You used to laugh in the shop sometimes, when Dorothy said something, and you'd try to hide it behind your tea mug." He glanced at her. "You weren't as subtle as you thought."

"I was completely subtle."

"Dorothy noticed too. She mentioned it to Linda. Linda mentioned it to Susan."

Diane pressed her fingers to her eyes. "I was being observed by a network."

"Affectionately observed."

"That's not better."

"It's a little better." Brian said with the utmost certainty and soft smile, the one that creases at his eyes, the smile Diane had been falling for since December, her favorite smile.

It was better. She knew it was better. She lowered her hand and looked at him across the small table and thought: four months ago, I did not know this person existed, and now I cannot imagine this town without him in it.

"Tell me something," she said.

"What kind of something?"

"Something I don't know yet. Something from before Ember Creek."

He turned his wine glass slowly. Thinking. She had learned to love this about him — the way he thought before he answered, the way he treated questions as things worth considering rather than prompts to be filled.

"When I was twenty-three," he said, "I built a bookshelf for my apartment, and it was so badly made that it collapsed in the middle of the night and took out half my book collection and a lamp."

"No!" Diane said. "And yet you went into carpentry?"

"In spite of. Or possibly because of. I was very motivated to never have a shelf collapse on me again."

She was smiling so much, her face hurt. "Okay. My turn. When I was twenty-six, I tried to make croissants from scratch for a dinner party, and they came out looking like — I do not have a kind comparison. Eddie called them 'architectural decisions.' We served them anyway and nobody said anything, which was somehow worse."

Brian's face did the thing — the full, genuine, surprised laugh. "Architectural decisions." He repeated.

"He kept one. On the windowsill. For three weeks. He said it had structural integrity."

She said it easily, the way she had been learning to say things about Eddie — not carefully, not around the edge of it, but straight through.

Brian did not flinch. Did not redirect. He just smiled — a warm, listening smile — and said: "He sounds like someone who understood you completely."

She looked at him from across the small table in the warm kitchen light.

"He did," she said. "He really did."

They were quiet for a moment.

"Tell me something else," Brian said. And they continued this pattern of conversation well into the night, neither of them paying any attention to the time, only each other.

They talked generously, each of them leaning slightly forward over the small table as the evening deepened outside, the wine level dropped, the breadbasket emptied and neither of them mentioned anything about leaving.

She told him about Portland in the autumn — the specific smell of it, the way the city went amber and red, and the coffee shops filled up and the whole place felt like a long exhale.

He told her about his mother, who called every Sunday and had an opinion about everything with the same cheerful authority as Susan, which he had only recently understood was not a coincidence. He told her about the furniture piece he was proudest of — a dining table he had built for a couple in Denver who had commissioned it for their twentieth anniversary, wide oak planks, hand-joined, the kind of table that was made to hold forty years of Sunday dinners.

"Brian," she said.

"Mm."

"Thank you for dinner."

He looked up from his glass. "We haven't had dessert."

"I know." She smiled. "I'm thanking you for the whole thing. The bad lamp story. The croissant sympathy. The table you made for the anniversary couple." She paused. "For asking if you could come on the walk this morning."

He was very still for a moment.

"Thank you," he said, "for answering."

They looked at each other across the small table in the warm kitchen light, and the evening was fully dark outside the window now and neither of them had noticed.

~

She should have left an hour ago.

She knew this and did nothing about it, because the kitchen was warm and the conversation had moved seamlessly from the table to the small living room where she'd ended up on the couch next to Brian, with her legs tucked under her and they were discussing, with a seriousness that they both understood was slightly absurd, whether the rooster situation had been handled correctly. Gerald had become quite the talk around the town as everyone supported the option to make Gerald a formal resident of Ember Creek which would go against town ordinance, but no one cared, Gerald was a part of the town, and we were all rooting for our newest feathered friend. #TeamGerald.

"The rose bush sound barrier is inspiring," Diane said. "Dorothy should have been a diplomat."

"Dorothy was a diplomat. Thirty-one years in a classroom is just diplomacy with smaller constituents."

"That's exactly right. Someone should tell her that!" Diane said excitedly.

"Someone should absolutely not tell her that. She would use it to justify every opinion she's ever had."

Diane laughed, Brian laughed, and the room was warm with it as their eyes met each other and stayed there as if they had nowhere else they needed to be.

"I should go," she said.

"Probably," he said but he did not move.

"It's almost eleven." Diane urged.

"It is." Brian said without any concern in his voice.

She unfolded herself from the couch and Brian walked with her over to the door. She gathered her cardigan and her bag, and they stepped out onto the front porch together into the June dark.

The night was extraordinary.

It was the kind of mountain night that happened in the deep heart of summer — warm enough to stand in without shivering, the air still carrying the day's heat from the rock faces but with the cool underneath it that the valley floor held after sunset. The sky above was crowded with stars that looked almost white in places. From somewhere down the street, the smell of someone's late-burning fire drifted past — cedar and pine, warm and sweet.

They stood on the porch for a moment, side by side, taking it all in.

"Look at that sky," she said softly, more to herself than to him.

"Every night," he said. "Every single night and it still does that to me."

They walked down the front steps and across the small yard to where her car sat at the curb, and she stopped with her hand on the door and turned to look at him — at Brian in the starlight, in the warm June air — and found that she didn't want to get in.

He was looking at her.

"I had a really good evening," she said.

"So did I."

"The pasta was good."

"The pasta was adequate. You do not have to—"

"Brian. The pasta was good."

He was smiling. She could see it even in the dark — the quality of his face when it was smiling, the way it changed everything around his eyes. She had memorized that smile for months.

"Today was—" she started.

"Yeah, it was" he interrupted.

"I keep thinking about the ridge. About this morning."

"So do I." Brian said softly.

"And then I come here and it's — it's easy, Brian. It is so easy with you. And I do not know why I am surprised by that. I have known it was easy for months. But tonight it felt—"

"Like something that was always meant to be?" he asked in a way that was telling and not really asking.

She looked at him. "Yes. Exactly like that."

He took a single step towards her.

She did not step back. She had been stepping back from things for two and a half years — away from the grief, away from the wanting, away from the kind of hope that could hurt you when it did not hold. She had been so careful. So, measured. So determined to protect what was left of her by keeping everything at a safe distance of manageable feeling.

With the urge to let go of the careful control she had been living under, she did. She let go.

She reached up and put both hands against his chest, entangled her fingers into his shirt, pulling him into her, dismantling the fear, and removing any room between them and as sure as the sun rises to the sky, her lips rose to his and she kissed him.

~

This kiss was different from the one on the ridge.

That one had been an answer — certain, warm, the resolution of a question months in the asking. This one was something else entirely. This one was the thing that came after the answer, the place the answer led to, the door that opened once you had stopped being afraid of what was behind it.

She kissed him with everything.

With the grief — all of it, the full weight of two and a half years of carrying something that had no bottom, of learning to walk with it, of waking up every morning and choosing to keep going even when keeping going felt like the bravest and most exhausting thing she had ever done.

With the loneliness — the specific, loneliness of a person who had been loved completely and then was not.

With the fear — the fear that had made her look away every time his eyes found hers, that had made her study hat displays and take very natural walks on the other side of the street and build elaborate internal arguments for why she wasn't curious about a man she was absolutely, undeniably curious about.

With the hope — the tentative hope that she had arrived in Ember Creek carrying. The hope that a mountain town and a corner armchair and a cup of chamomile tea might be enough to begin the long slow work of finding her way back to herself.

She kissed him with all of it. Every single piece. She gave it to him not as a burden but as the most honest thing she had — the whole of herself, the broken, the healing, the still-uncertain and the newly brave — and he received it the way he received everything: completely, without flinching, with his hands holding her face and then her shoulders and then moving to her back and drawing her in until there was no space left between them.

He kissed her back just as fully.

He kissed her with his eight months of being okay and knowing it was not enough. With the quiet apartment in Denver and the two years of fine. With the January market, the hat booth, the fence gap and all the near-misses he had carried home and set down gently in the dark of his house and tried not to look at too closely.

He kissed her with the certainty of a man who had built things that lasted and knew, bone-deep, the difference between something constructed hastily and something made to hold.

This, Diane, was made to hold.

When they finally pulled back — both catching their breath, her hands gripping the front of his flannel the same way they had on the ridge, his forehead coming to rest against hers.

"Diane," he said.

Just her name. But the way he said it — low and a little undone, like a man who has arrived somewhere he did not entirely trust he was going to reach — made her eyes fill.

She did not let the tears fall. She just blinked them back and breathed and let her forehead stay where it was, against his.

"I know," she said.

~

He put his arms around her.

Both arms coming around her and drawing her fully against him, one hand between her shoulder blades and one at the back of her head, and he held her in the warm June dark beneath the mountain stars.

He was making room.

He was not just holding Diane — he was holding everything she came with. All the grief and the history and the two and a half years of learning to carry something heavy without letting it crush her.

He was holding all of it, deliberately, as if to say: I have arms big enough. My heart is open. I am not going anywhere.

She felt it.

She let herself be held.

She had been holding herself upright for so long. Through the accident and the arrangements and the first terrible year and the second quieter one. Through the decision to leave Portland and the drive up the mountain and the moving truck and Pete's careful, worried eyes. Through every morning, she had gotten up and made coffee and gone out into the pines and told herself that starting over was possible even when she was not sure she believed it.

She had held herself up through all of it.

And now — here — she let herself put some of the weight down.

She turned her face into his chest. She felt his arms tighten slightly. She felt his lips press gently to the top of her head, the same way they had on the ridge, the same simple and unhurried tenderness, and she thought: *this is the best version of the story.*

She had not known, until this moment, how much she had missed this.

Not the romance of it — though that too, yes, the warmth of being wanted by someone who had chosen her. But this. Just this. The fundamental, irreducible comfort of being held by someone who meant it. Of not having to be the only one keeping yourself standing.

She felt the grief move through her, gently.

Not painfully — not the way it had come in the first year, in waves that knocked her sideways and left her breathless on the bathroom floor. Just a gentle moving-through, like a current of air through a room that has been closed too long. A last loosening of something she had been gripping without knowing she was gripping it.

Eddie.

And then — quietly, from somewhere inside her, from whatever place held the things that were permanent —

she heard him.

Not a sound. Not a voice she could have described to anyone who asked. But unmistakably, entirely, specifically him — the warmth of him, the humor of him, the way he had always known what she needed before she had worked it out herself:

This is the best version of the story, Di.

She closed her eyes as she felt the tears building again.

She pressed her cheek more firmly against Brian's chest. Felt his arms hold her closer in response, wordless and immediate, as though he could feel that something had just moved through her.

One breath.

Then another.

Then a third.

She lifted her head.

She looked up at Brian — at his face in the starlight, at the blue eyes she had memorized from across a dozen rooms.

"Are you all right?" he said softly.

She took a breath and smiled as she answered.

"Yes," she said. "I really am."

And it was the truest thing she had said in two and a half years.

Not performing fine. Not managing okay. Not surviving the current stretch until the next one. But genuinely, with her whole self and nothing held back: All right.

Brian looked at her for a long moment. Then he did something she had not expected — he smiled, slowly, in the way he had when something genuinely pleased him, the smile that started at the edges of his eyes before it reached his mouth.

"Good," he said. Simply. Like it was the only word required.

~

She drove home through the mountain dark with the windows down, the stars overhead and the lightness of someone who has set something down that they have been carrying too long.

She parked in front of the cabin. She sat for a moment with the engine off, the night pressing warmly in through the open windows.

She thought about Eddie's voice — the warmth of it, the specific rightness of it. The way it had arrived was not as grief but as a gift. The way it had felt not like loss revisited but like something released.

The best version of the story.

She looked at the cabin, at the lavender on the porch railing, barely visible in the dark but there, at the light she had left on in the kitchen, warm and yellow in the window, and at the life she had assembled here, piece by piece, since November.

In this moment, Diane realized her story was a story worth continuing to write.

She had not always believed that. There had been months — long months, grey months, the specific months of winter that came after the accident — when she had believed, quietly and without telling anyone, that the best of her story was behind her. That the chapter with the love in it was over. That what remained was something less — manageable, decent, and survivable, but less.

She had been wrong.

Diane got out of her car and began walking up her front steps but this time it was different. She was not walking into another night of loss, loneliness and thoughts that haunted her, no. Instead, for the first time since losing Eddie, she was walking into her story, the one with the best version that she did not think was possible. She took a deep breath as she opened her door and stepped inside to a new chapter.

She made tea, she picked up her book and curled up in the armchair by the window as the fire glowed and she read.

As she read, she realized she was not just reading stories again, she was back to writing her own and finally believing that

her story was not over, that it was just
beginning.

Chapter 20

The Book on the Shelf

In July, Diane opened Eddie's box for the last time.

She took the books out one by one and put them on her shelf — the shelf she had built, finally, for the overflow from her growing collection. The shelf Brian had installed for her one Saturday morning while she read instructions to him from her chair in a voice doing a deliberately bad impression of a flight attendant.

He had laughed, kept building, and got it perfectly right.

She arranged Eddie's books alongside her own, not separate. Mixed in with everything else — the books she had read since November, the new ones that kept arriving, and the ones she had borrowed from Susan's collection. The whole shelf was her, now. All of it.

She kept the box.

She folded it flat and put it in the back of the closet, where it would always be findable. She was not finished with it. She did not think she ever would be, and she had made peace with that. Some things do not close; they just get carried differently.

There was one book that had Eddie's handwriting in it — the one with the checkmarks and the margin notes. She put it at eye level, in the middle of the shelf, where it could be easily reached. She did not read it. She was not ready for that yet. Maybe next year or even, the year after that.

She had time.

~

Brian came over that afternoon and found her on the porch in an expression that people who knew her had learned to recognize — present but inward, the look of someone who has been somewhere tender and came back.

"You okay?" he asked.

"Yes," she said. "I did a thing, come inside, I want to show you" she said with excitement.

Brian stepped up to the porch and followed Diane inside.

When they walked inside Diane pointed to the shelf. He looked at it for a moment, studying the layout and order of the books.

"The one in the middle," he said.

"Eddie's handwriting." Diane softly whispered.

He nodded. He did not say anything, which was the right thing, because he understood by now that some moments were not requests for responses.

Diane smiled and turned to walk back outside onto the porch and invited Brian to join her.

They sat on the porch in the July afternoon; the mountain was enormous and green. Her lavender seedling had taken root in the pot by the railing and was beginning to bloom. The whole valley below them was full of summer.

"I want to tell you something," she said.

"Okay."

"I started reading romance novels again. Properly. All the way through."

He turned to look at her. He knew what this meant. She had told him, over the months, about the box and the bookshelf and the two years of not reading.

"I used to think they were just stories," she said. "After Eddie. I thought — real love doesn't get a happy ending, so what's the point of stories that say it does." She looked at the mountain. "But I think I was wrong about what a happy ending means. I think it does not mean anything ever hurts or nothing is ever lost. I think it means — you keep going. You come back. You find something worth finding."

"Yeah," Brian said quietly.

"I think the books were right all along. I just wasn't reading them correctly."

He reached over and took her hand.

"What are you reading now?" he asked.

"A new one. Susan sent it with you last week." Diane smirked as she looked over to Brian, "Susan said you had to read it."

"I'm not going to argue with Susan." Brian said as he halfway rolled his eyes realizing that he was now going to have two women in his life entangling him in their romance reading. He smiled, gently, and thought: Bring on the entanglement!

"No one has ever successfully argued with Susan."

They both sat with the mountain and silence coming to know, together, that this was the beginning of their very own romance story.

~

The Book Nook had a new display in the window by August. Linda had made it herself, with the small handwritten cards she used for her favorites. In the center of the display was a chair — the armchair from the back corner, moved to the window — and on the seat was a mug and an open book. The card in the window, visible from the street, read: "Every great story begins with someone brave enough to turn the first page."

Dorothy said it was the best window display Linda had ever done.

Diane knew that window display was created because of her. Every day she admired the display as a reminder of moving to Ember Creek, meeting Linda and how her story began a new chapter because she had turned the page.

~

On a Saturday in late August, Diane worked the morning shift, and at noon Brian came in with lunch from Ruby's — two brown bags, no announcement, which was how they did most things now.

They ate in the back corner. Her corner. The gossip was good that day. The rooster situation had finally, after nine months of community deliberation, reached a resolution involving a formal agreement and a sound barrier made of rose bushes, which Dorothy described as "a diplomatic triumph."

Brian listened to the rooster update with an expression of complete engagement. He had strong feelings about the rooster.

He had since January. She told him everything she had gathered from the corner, all of it, every season's worth, and he had been a worthy audience.

He caught her eye over his sandwich.

She caught his over her tea.

The bell above the door rang — ding ding — and they both looked up. A woman came in with a child on her hip, new to the shop, looking around with the slightly overwhelmed expression of someone encountering too much at once.

"Welcome to The Book Nook," Diane said warmly. "Can I help you find something?"

The woman smiled. "I just moved to town, and someone told me this was the place to start."

Diane stood up. Across the table, Brian was smiling — that small, just-for-her smile.

"It is," she said. "It absolutely is."

~

That evening, she sat on the porch with a book open on her lap and the mountain ahead of her. The light was slowly going gold and then rose and then the particular blue of a mountain dusk that she had come to love more than any city sunset she had ever seen.

She had called Pete earlier that afternoon. She had told him about the shelf, the lavender, an update on Brian, the rooster situation, and its resolution.

"Diane," Pete had said.

"What?"

"You sound like you." Pete had paused. "You sound more like you than you have in a long time and it's really good to hear."

She went quiet for a moment.

"Yeah," she had said. "I think I do, too."

Pete and Diane spoke well into the early evening as they always did. After the catch up of Ember Creek drama and life events, they said their goodnights and Diane hung up.

Diane sat on her porch into the evening with her book and thought about Eddie — she thought about him every day, would think about him every day, and had made a gentle peace with the fact that this was not a problem to be solved but a love to be honored.

She looked at the mountain and she thought about Brian, the one who had become part of the story that was becoming the best version.

Brian texted "Has your lavender bloomed yet? Susan is asking."

"Almost," she had texted back. "Come see."

She heard his truck on the mountain road realizing he had already been on his way before texting her.

She turned to page two.

The pines moved in the evening wind. The valley held its light a little longer. The mountain was enormous, patient, and good — not rushing anything, trusting that the things worth having will arrive when they are ready.

She was, at last, exactly where her story needed to be.

Diane looked up and there he was, Brian, walking up the gravel drive to her with that smile she loved, and she let out a sigh and thought, this is it, the very best version of her story.

~ Ember Creek ~

Epilogue

On a sunny afternoon in the dead heat of July, Dorothy made her way to the mailbox like she did every single day.

Since retiring, Dorothy had formed quite the routine for herself — because she had learned, in retirement, that one must maintain a routine or life gets unnecessarily boring. Every morning without exception she went to Ruby's for the cinnamon rolls that everyone in Ember Creek adored and that Dorothy had never once pretended she didn't need. By mid-morning she made her way to The Book Nook right at opening, where she would investigate the romance section with the focused intensity of someone on a scavenger hunt, as though there was a reasonable possibility that Linda had snuck in a new novel without telling her. Dorothy knew good and well that no such surprise existed on the shelves. It was simply her cover for being at the shop every day without feeling out of place — and Linda, who knew everything, had never once said so.

Linda always had the chamomile tea hot and ready, and Dorothy had grown a warm place in her heart for that cup. It was comfort in a mug, and it was reliable, and at seventy-one, Dorothy had developed a deep appreciation for both.

At three o'clock sharp, she ventured down her driveway after watching the postal carrier make his pass. She wasn't expecting much — the monthly newsletter, perhaps, and the usual assortment of things she hadn't asked for and didn't want. She opened the mailbox and found three pieces inside. The newsletter, right on schedule, an advertisement from the hardware store, and an envelope.

The envelope was the size of a card. On the back was a wax seal — she turned it over and found lavender pressed into the wax, neat and deliberate. Dorothy blinked. She flipped the envelope over and squinted at the front, wishing she had remembered her glasses, and then her eyes went wide.

The handwriting was the most beautiful she had ever seen on a piece of mail. And in the return address, in that careful, unhurried script:

Brian and Diane.

Dorothy did not hesitate. She turned on her heel and headed back to The Book Nook.

She had never gone in during the afternoon rush — that was a firm and longstanding personal policy — but this was not a usual afternoon, and this was not a usual letter, and personal policies, Dorothy had always believed, existed to be set aside when the circumstances genuinely warranted it.

She hustled around the corner, down two blocks, and pushed open the dark green door with a force that sent the bell into considerably more than two rings, bringing every person inside to a sudden and complete halt.

Dorothy stopped just inside the doorway and worked to catch her breath. She scanned the room.

Almost all of Ember Creek was already there.

And every single one of them was holding a white envelope exactly like the one in her hands.

Dorothy's chest was heaving. Her heart was racing. Across the room, Linda's eyes found hers, and Linda was smiling the way the morning sun smiled — wide and warm and entirely inevitable. Just below where Linda stood, the white ceramic vase sat on the counter with its sprig of lavender.

Dorothy looked up at her. "How?"

Linda's smile stretched further.

"Wait —" Dorothy tried again, still catching her breath. "When? How?"

Linda shook her head gently. "I just knew."

"Of course you did!" Dorothy exclaimed, and then she laughed — a full, real laugh that came up through the tears that had snuck out without her permission, because Dorothy did not cry at announcements, and yet here she was, doing exactly that, and she found she didn't mind at all.

Linda's own eyes had gone bright. She watched the joy and disbelief wash over Dorothy's face and settle there, and she felt her heart fill with something she didn't quite have a word for — only that it was right, and that it had been a long time coming, and that she was very glad to be in this room on this particular afternoon.

The arrival of the engagement was welcomed by every soul in Ember Creek.

Later, Dorothy would plant both hands on the counter and say to no one in particular: "How did they keep that a secret? No one has managed to keep anything a secret in this town since 1989."

Linda laughed. "I don't know. But I think we all knew, in our own way."

Dorothy nodded slowly, the envelope still in her hand. "You know what the most extraordinary part is? They sent these to all of us — at the same time, so we would all receive them on the same day. Not one person was going to have this without the whole town having it."

The creases around Linda's eyes deepened. "And that, Dorothy, I believe is the most thoughtful thing anyone has ever done for this town."

It had taken the town a full year to arrive at this day. But what a year it had been.

Since the formal confirmation of Brian and Diane as a couple the previous June, the days in Ember Creek had continued much as they always did — and yet they were different in the way that a room is different when the right lamp is turned on. The love between them brought something extra to each ordinary day that the whole town felt and quietly enjoyed. The space Ember Creek had always made for two singular people now made room for the companionship

294

between them, and the town settled into that new shape the way it settled into everything: warmly, without fuss, as though it had always been the plan.

Which, of course, it had.

Their mornings began on the trail. Brian brought coffee in the oldest thermos Diane had ever seen — a battered, dented thing that looked as though it had spent a decade on a construction site and had come to terms with its own mortality. She teased him about it almost every morning.

"Let me guess," she would say, already grinning before the words were out. "You brought the coffee coffin."

Brian would laugh, low and easy. "Hey. This thing keeps coffee hotter than anything else you'll ever find. I'll keep it, and you'll keep getting hot coffee. Everybody wins."

She would nudge him with her elbow and then wrap her arm around his waist, and they would start up the trail — sometimes talking the whole way, sometimes walking in silence with their hands threaded together, and it was perfect either way. Those walks became her favorite part of every day. Not for any single thing they said or did, but for the simple, reliable fact of them. The coffee. The mountain. The man beside her.

Their evenings found their own rhythm too. "Your place or mine?" became the standing mid-afternoon text — the daily confirmation that the evening ahead was theirs and would be spent together. She would arrive at his door in her comfy clothes, usually with a book in one hand

and either groceries or takeout from Ruby's in the other. Each evening brought laughter and conversation and a closeness that both of them had forgotten was possible and were grateful, every day, to have found again.

~

While love was very much in the air on one side of Ember Creek, the opposite was briefly, chaotically true for Gerald.

In November, there was a development on Millbrook Lane that the town would discuss for considerably longer than was strictly necessary — and which provided the cold-weather entertainment that the rooster situation, in its newly resolved state, had previously been supplying.

It began, as most things in Ember Creek began, with a noise.

Specifically, a noise at four-fifteen in the morning that was not Gerald's customary crow — not the single, authoritative announcement that had been the subject of formal petition and counter-petition and nine months of procedural delay. Three households on the east side of Millbrook Lane described it, in the second formal noise complaint filed in as many years, as "chaotic," "layered," "distressing in its variety," and — in Dorothy's addendum to the filing — "frankly unprecedented in both volume and character."

The rose bush sound barrier, it emerged, had been a perfectly effective solution to the Gerald problem as originally constituted. What it had not accounted for — what no one had anticipated, and what Doug Martinson had notably failed to disclose during nine months of community deliberation — was that Patsy Martinson had, at some point in the late summer, acquired hens. Six of them, to be exact.

Gerald, who had spent the better part of a year as the sole and sovereign voice of the Martinson property, had initially received this development with the baffled, wary energy of a man who has lived alone for a long time and isn't quite sure what to do with company. He had adjusted. He had, by all observable evidence, begun to consider his situation improved.

The problem, which became apparent on the Tuesday morning in question, was one of proportion.

Six hens, it turned out, were too many hens for Gerald.

The details, as reconstructed by Ruby from the accounts of three eyewitnesses and one extremely animated phone call from Patsy Martinson herself, were these: Gerald had apparently attempted, at four-fifteen in the morning, to assert some form of order over the coop. The hens — who were six in number and had collectively decided that Gerald's authority was more theoretical than practical — had disagreed. With feeling. With coordination. With what Ruby described, with evident admiration, as "a level of organizational sophistication that I find frankly impressive in a hen."

Gerald had fled.

This was what the three households found most remarkable when they looked out their windows at four-sixteen in the morning — the sight of Gerald, heritage breed Wyandotte rooster of documented lineage, running the full length of the Martinson property at a speed nobody had previously associated with him, cackling in a register that was less the confident crow of a sovereign bird and more the urgent commentary of an individual in genuine distress, pursued at close range by six hens who had reached a collective limit and were making their position emphatically known.

The rose bushes, installed specifically to contain sound, contained none of this.

Dorothy filed the complaint herself — with mixed feelings, by her own admission. She had been pro-petition from the beginning and felt structurally vindicated by this development, but she had also developed, over the course of the year, a complicated and reluctant affection for Gerald that she had not predicted. She described her emotional state in the filing as "conflicted but clear-eyed."

Two days after the incident, Doug Martinson appeared at The Book Nook — which everyone agreed was either very brave or very misguided — and informed Linda that Patsy would be reducing the flock to two hens, which Gerald had handled previously without incident, and that the matter would not recur. Linda made him a chamomile tea and said she was glad to hear it.

Gerald was not available for comment. He had been, according to Patsy, unusually quiet since Tuesday, and had taken to sitting on the far side of the coop with his back to the door in a posture she described as "reflective", and Dorothy described as "the look of a bird reconsidering his choices."

Since the reduction of the flock, Gerald had slowly returned to himself — the bright, feathered, occasionally insufferable version of himself that the whole town had come to love. Diane, with characteristic warmth, suggested that Patsy find a pet counselor to ensure no permanent emotional damage had been sustained. The town took this seriously, because Ember Creek took Gerald seriously, and because after everything he had been through, he deserved to be asked how he was doing.

~

Brian had known he wanted to marry Diane from the morning on the ridge in June when he had finally opened his heart and taken the step to fit into hers.

Diane was not someone he saw as ordinary. She was one of a kind — his kind — and he wanted to keep her for always. But he had also learned, over the months since that morning, that patience was not just something Diane needed — it was something she deserved. She had given what room she could find in her heart to him, and he understood that opening the door to love was the easy part. It was walking the path of a second chance that he wanted to allow her, at her own pace. She was worth waiting for. As long as she needed, Brian was going to be right where he said he would be.

She told him in February.

Not in words. In the way she said his name one morning — just his name, just Brian, the two syllables she'd said a thousand times, but with a quality in them he hadn't heard before. Full. Without reservation. Without the faint, careful holding-back that had lived in everything for the first months while she was still finding her way. He looked up from his coffee. She was looking at him across the kitchen table with an expression he would carry for the rest of his life.

He knew then that he wasn't waiting anymore.

He planned it for June. Exactly one year from the morning they had stood on the ridge, and the valley had been wide open below them. Their spot — the place where the trees thinned and the whole mountain opened, where the bird with the three descending notes lived in the pines, where the mist burned off the valley floor every morning and the day declared itself. It was the only place it could possibly be.

He didn't tell anyone. This surprised him, later — that he had managed it, that he had carried the plan through four months of Ember Creek without a single person knowing. He had bought the ring in March, from a jeweler in a mountain town two hours south and brought it home and put it in the drawer of his workbench. He had taken it out sometimes in the evenings, just to look at it. Just to feel the weight of what it meant.

On a Sunday morning in June, he asked Diane if she wanted to take their usual walk. She looked at the morning — at the pale gold of the sky, the clean sharpness of the high-altitude air — and said yes. She put on her green linen dress and laced her boots. When they stepped outside and started toward the trail, she took his hand the way she always did, her fingers finding his without looking, the easy habit of two people who have learned each other completely.

The trail climbed. The pines thinned. Below them, the valley held the last of the morning mist — the same mist, the same pines, the same mountain as a year ago. Enormous and patient and good.

At the ridge, he stopped.

She stopped beside him and turned to look. Something in the way he was standing — the stillness of him, the quality of his attention — made her go still too.

He reached into the pocket of his jacket.

He was not a man who made speeches. He had thought about what to say for four months and had arrived, in the end, at the simplest version — the one most true, the one with no performance in it. Just him. What he meant. What he was asking.

He looked at her, and he knelt down on one knee.

"I want to keep showing up," he said. "For the rest of it. All of it. Every Thursday and every porch evening and every morning on this mountain and everything that comes after. I want to be the person who shows up for you, Diane. For all of you. For everything you carry and everything you're still finding." He stopped. "Will you let me?"

He held up the ring.

"Diane, will you marry me?"

She stood very still and looked at him.

She thought of the ridge a year ago — the morning that had started everything, the valley below them, her own voice saying there is *absolutely room*. She thought of the box and the shelf and the book with the handwriting in the margins. She thought of Eddie — warmly, completely, with the full and permanent love of someone who is carried rather than lost — and she felt him, in the way she always did. Not as absence. As presence. Not as grief. As a gift.

This is the best version of the story, Di.

Keep writing it.

She looked at Brian — at the blue eyes and the morning light and the ring in his hand and the entirety of the last year written on his face. All the Thursdays and the porch evenings and the October Sunday when he had sat beside her and said nothing and been exactly the right thing.

"Yes," she said.

She said it again, because it deserved to be said twice.

"Yes."

He put the ring on her finger with steady hands — he was always steady — warm and slightly rough and entirely certain. He held her face the way he had on the ridge a year ago and kissed her, and the mountain held them both the way it always had — enormous and patient, the perfect witness to the importance of this one small, extraordinary life.

~

Back in The Book Nook on that Tuesday in July, Dorothy was still holding the announcement.

The room had filled until there was barely space to move, and Linda had propped the green door open to let in the summer air and make room for whoever was still arriving. In Ember Creek, that was simply how it worked. Good news came and the town gathered — not because anyone organized it or sent an invitation, but because gathering was what this family did when something mattered. No instruction required.

Carla had stopped crying and started making a list of things that needed organizing, which was her love language. Beth had called her sister. Tom Kettley had quietly rearranged three shelves of books because he needed something to do with his hands. Henry Baker was telling anyone within earshot that honey was a traditional wedding gift in fourteen different cultures — which may or may not have been accurate, but nobody argued.

Ruby had gone back to the diner and returned with a full pot of coffee, because she understood that news of this magnitude required caffeine, and because Ruby Baker had never once arrived at a significant moment without exactly what was needed. She stood by the window and looked out at Main Street.

Dorothy came to stand beside her.

They stood together without speaking, watching the ordinary and extraordinary afternoon of a small mountain town that had been holding its people for a hundred and forty years and fully intended to go on.

"I knew," Ruby said.

"You always know," Dorothy said.

"December," Ruby said. "The way he looked at the door."

"The hat booth," Dorothy replied. "January market. He stood there looking at those hats for eleven full minutes. That man has never cared about a hat in his life."

Ruby glanced at her sideways, "You timed him?"

"I noted the duration," Dorothy said with great precision. "There is a meaningful distinction."

Ruby smiled into her coffee. Dorothy grinned. They both knew Dorothy was completely full of it, and both of them enjoyed it enormously.

The afternoon light came through the open green door and lay across the wooden floors in the way it did at this hour — warm and low and golden, the light of a day that had been good and knew it. The lavender in the white ceramic vase leaned toward it. The armchair in the window, which had held Diane through a full mountain winter and into the summer of her new beginning, sat open and available — the way something sits when it has done its work and is ready, patiently, for whoever needs it next.

Linda looked at all of it.

She thought about the years she had spent in this shop, in this town, watching love find people in the unhurried way it always found them in Ember Creek. She thought about how love had found her here too, a long time ago — had given her years she still carried, quietly, every day. She knew what Brian and Diane were walking toward. She knew the kind of life that was waiting. And she couldn't think of two people more deserving of every moment of it.

Ember Creek had done its work. It always did.

The bell rang — ding ding — and Susan Henderson came through the door.

She moved carefully, the way she always did since the hip — deliberate and dignified, at her own pace, and no one was going to rush her. Brian had driven her down from the mountain road and was parking the truck. She had not waited.

She came inside and looked at the room — at all of them, this town, this community that had held her grandson and the woman he loved through the irreplaceable year just passed — and she was quiet for a moment.

Her eyes found the lavender vase.

She pressed both hands to her chest.

Then she looked at Linda — across twenty-three years of book orders and chamomile tea and the long, patient work of a woman who arranged things by feeling and was very rarely wrong.

"Thank you," Susan said. Simply. Entirely.

Linda nodded. The look between them held everything that needed to be said.

The bell rang again — ding ding — and the whole room turned.

Brian and Diane walked in together.

Hand in hand. The summer light behind them. Diane in her green linen dress, Brian in his work clothes with the easy, unhurried certainty of a man who is exactly where he is supposed to be. They stepped inside, and as their eyes adjusted from the brightness of the afternoon, they took in the room — every face, every glowing expression, every white envelope held in every pair of hands.

Before either of them could speak, before they could take another step, the whole room went up.

Cheering and tears and arms reaching and voices all at once — the unrepeatable sound of a community that loves two people and has been waiting a very long time to say so at full volume. Hugs pulled close and held long. Laughter running through the crying. Love, loud and uncontained, filling every corner of The Book Nook on a Tuesday afternoon in July.

Diane made her way to Linda through the crowd. Linda opened her arms and held her — not briefly, not politely, but fully, the way you hold someone when you have been quietly, steadfastly rooting for them since the moment they walked through your door. When they finally stepped back, Diane's eyes were bright. She turned toward the display in the front window — the armchair, the open book, the afternoon light — and noticed the card.

"Is that a new card?" she asked.

Linda smiled. "That it is my sweet girl."

Diane walked to the window and read it.

> *Every great story begins with someone brave enough to turn the first page.*

She stood there for a moment, with the summer light coming through the green door and the sound of her whole town behind her and the ring on her finger catching the afternoon gold.

She thought about the woman who had walked through this door in November with cold mountain air on her coat. She thought about the corner armchair, the chamomile tea, the bell that had rung twice and let her in.

She thought about everything that had come after.

She turned back to the room — to Brian across the crowd, watching her with that smile. The one she had been cataloguing since December and would spend the rest of her life admiring.

She smiled back.

She had come here to start over.

She had found something so much better than that — she had found the best version of the story.

And she was living in every word of it.

~ Ember Creek ~

A Note from the Author

Ember Creek is not a real place.

But the longing for it is.

Several years ago, I moved to a small mountain town with a heart full of hope and a very specific dream of what that life was going to look like. I had imagined something like Ember Creek — warm and eccentric and full of people who would make room for a newcomer without being asked. People who would hand you a cup of tea and learn your order and argue loudly about a rooster and fold you, eventually, into the fabric of their community.

What I found was something else entirely.

Cold shoulders. Distances I couldn't cross no matter how hard I tried. The loneliness of being surrounded by people who simply didn't have space for one more. It was hard in a way I hadn't expected and wasn't prepared for, and I carried that disappointment for a long time — the gap between the town I had imagined and the town I had actually found.

Ember Creek is what I wished that experience had been like.

It is the welcome I wanted. The community I dreamed of. The green door I hoped I would walk through and find someone like Linda on the other side, already knowing how I took my tea. I wrote this town into existence because I needed it to exist somewhere, even if only on the page — and in writing it, I found that I loved it so completely that I couldn't bear to leave.

I hope you couldn't either.

~

I chose to write romance because I love, love.

That is the simplest and most honest thing I can tell you about why this book exists. I am a hopeless romantic in the truest sense of the word — not naive about love, not unaware of how hard it can be, but deeply and stubbornly convinced that it is the most worth-writing-about thing in the world. Joy is my deepest place. Love is where I live. And I wanted to write from there.

But I also wanted to write something true about grief.

Because I think we get grief wrong sometimes. We talk about it as something to get over — a mountain to climb and descend and leave behind. We measure recovery by distance, as though the goal is to one day look back and feel nothing.

That is not what I believe. And it is not what Diane believes, either.

Grief, at its truest, is not the absence of love. It is love with nowhere left to go — love that outlasts the person it was made for and has to learn, slowly and imperfectly, to be carried rather than set down. The heart doesn't shrink after loss. It stretches. It makes room. And one of the most courageous things a person can do — one of the bravest pages anyone can turn — is to allow new love into a heart that has already loved deeply and lost.

That is Diane's story. And I hope, in some small way, it speaks to you.

~

If you are reading this and you have ever stood at the edge of something new and been afraid — afraid to want it, afraid to lose it, afraid that wanting it again meant forgetting what you had before — I wrote this book for you.

Grief is not something you get over. It is someone you carry. And carrying them does not mean there is no room for anyone else. It means your heart has already proven it knows how to love something completely. That is not a wound. That is a gift.

Give yourself permission to keep writing.

The best version of your story may be the one that's still coming.

~

To every reader who found their way to Ember Creek — thank you.

You made this town real. You sat in the corner armchair. You took Linda's chamomile and Dorothy's opinions and Ruby's cinnamon rolls and the entire, ongoing Gerald situation and you carried all of it with you, and I am so grateful.

If I ever have to move to a small mountain town again, I can only hope it turns out to be somewhere like this.

A place with a green door.

A bell that rings twice.

And people who were already glad you came.

With so much love,
Elle Laine

Acknowledgment

To Kai Degraff —

You gave Ember Creek its face.

*The green door and the warmth of
everything this story holds—*

you saw it before anyone else could,

*and you put it exactly where it needed
to be.*

*Thank you for your extraordinary
talent, your patience, and your care.*

*This cover is everything I dreamed it
would be and more.*

With deep gratitude,
Elle Laine

THE PINKY PROMISE

A Novel

*Hope and Nathan made a pinky promise
on graduation night.*

*Two best friends. Two different states.
One unbreakable bond*

*that survived the miles, the years, and the
losses*

neither of them saw coming.

Life has a funny way of working out.

Pinky promises and all.

~

*Friends to Lovers · Slow Burn · Second Chances
Grief & Loss · Forced Proximity*

Coming July 18th, 2026

www.ingramcontent.com/pod-product-compliance
Lightning Source LLC
Chambersburg PA
CBHW071553150726
48000CB00004B/1451